THE
Mirrovr of Maiestie:

OR

THE BADGES OF HONOVR

Conceitedly Emblazoned.

A PHOTO-LITH FAC-SIMILE REPRINT
From Mr. Corser's perfect Copy.
A.D. 1618.

EDITED BY

HENRY GREEN, M.A., *and* JAMES CROSTON.

Published for the Holbein Society by
A. BROTHERS, *St. Ann's Square, Manchester;* and
TRÜBNER & CO., *Paternoster Row, London.*
M.DCCC.LXX.

To

The Rev. Thomas Corser, M.A. F.S.A. &c.

Vicar of Stand, Lancashire,

IN ADMIRATION

Of his high Scholarship in the old English Literature,

and

Of the marvellous Liberality with which he has communicated

of his skilfully gathered Treasures:

FROM THE EDITORS

of the Mirrovr of Maiestie.

M.DCCC.LXX.

PREFACE.

HE Mirrovr of Maiestie itself and the Photolith Plates annexed for illustration, supply good examples of the proper office of the Photographer, as an artist in fac-simile reprints. The Arms and Emblems of this work, as well as the letter-press, were, at first, in 1618, of defective execution, without finish in the woodcuts, and without sharpness or shapeliness in the type. Such faults might be urged as reasons for not reproducing the volume; but then its extreme rarity and the nature of its contents plead in

b

behalf of making the possession of a copy attainable at a moderate price.*

Shall the work be sent out honestly in its original homeliness? or shall meretricious graces be imparted to it by the hands of skilled engravers and typefounders? Let those who prefer it adopt the latter course, and as Pope did with Chaucer, let them modernize a WIFE OF BATH, and, despoiling her of her old-fashioned simplicity, bring to a too prurient fancy the questionable aid of a more mellifluous versification. Chaucer in his ancient roughness is far better than Pope in his modern polish.

The function of the photographer is not to coax natural blemishes into artificial beauties, nor to touch up antiquity and bestow an adventitious value on works of old; but with all exactness and care to set forth those works as they existed in the former days. He is indeed to seek out the best possible exemplars, and to bestow his highest skill on the fac-simile copy, occasionally concealing gross delineation by the transference of a more

* The copy from which our fac-simile was taken obtained by auction the high price of £36.

delicate design, and where lines or borders are evidently broken, restoring what once certainly existed; but he is not to use the appliances of modern art to elaborate a finished picture; the *truthful reproduction* ought to be his chief aim,— indeed his pride.

For want of bearing this principle in mind, some critics, otherwise well qualified, have widely erred by condemning as blemishes the truthful delineations which photo-lithography has presented of the engraver's and typographer's art in bygone times. Accuracy we hold to be essential to whatever claims approval as a fac-simile copy. It would often be very easy to surpass the original,— to aim at a higher style of art, and to give letter-press of a very superior character. For instance, in the illustrative plates, Nos. 1 and 16, the designs and the drawings might be considerably improved by the free employment of the graver's tools; and in plates 36–40, the much-worn letter-press of the original might have been set up in newest and sharpest type; but so to surpass would be to mislead. In fact, it would be unfair towards the Members of our Society, and towards literary men in general, who suppose that in our volume there has been supplied to them an exact reprint, truthful in letter and in line.

We heed not, then, those who in the spirit of insufficient knowledge thus criticise our photo-lithography; they do it, we doubt not, chiefly in their pride of admiration and love for the beautiful, and not through any superfluity of naughtiness towards our enterprise.

Our plan is to endeavour to obtain the best exemplars, and where practicable, as it often is, several of them, that the defects of one may be supplied by the excellencies of the others. With these exemplars the photo-lithographic proofs are closely compared, and unless the workmanship be good and skilful, other proofs are taken before the editors give forth the *imprimatur*. By following such a plan, it is not without hope of approval that we commend the Third of our Holbein Society's fac-simile reprints to the subscribers and to the public.

H. G. & J. C.

MANCHESTER, *Nov.* 1, 1870.

TABLE OF CONTENTS.

	Pages.
TITLE-PAGE and DEDICATION for the Fac-simile Reprint	i—iv
Preface	v—viii
Table of Contents, &c.	ix—xii
THE MIRROVR OF MAIESTIE, or the Badges of Honovr, viz.—	
Title-page.	
A CATALOGVE of those names vnto whom this worke is appropriated.	pp. 4
Dedication To THOSE NOBLE Personages rancked in the CATALOGVE.	
ARMS AND EMBLEMS	1–63
Forty Photo-lith Fac-simile Plates in Illustration, numbered 1—40	pp. 32

INTRODUCTION.

I. A BRIEF REVIEW of English Emblem-books previous to A.D. 1618, and of the Mirrovr of Maiestie itself	65–96
II. ANNOTATIONS on the Armorial Bearings and Noble Personages	97–159
III. NOTICES of similar Works, and especially of those from which the Illustrated Plates have been taken	160–174
GENERAL INDEX	175–180

THE

MIRROVR OF MAIESTIE,

AND

Forty

PHOTO-LITH FAC-SIMILE PLATES

in Illustration

of the Mirrovr of Maiestie.

———

M.DCCC.LXX.

THE MIRROVR
OF
MAIESTIE:
OR,
THE BADGES OF HONOVR
CONCEITEDLY EMBLAZONED;

WITH

EMBLEMES ANNEXED,
POETICALLY VNFOLDED.

——— *Nec his Plebecula gaudet.*

LONDON,
Printed by *W. I.* 1618.

A CATALOGVE OF THOSE NAMES VNTO WHOM this worke is appropriated.

THE Kings Maiestie.
The Queene.
The Prince.
The Lord Arch-Bishop of Canterburie.
The Lord Chancellor.
The Lord Treasurer.
The Lord Priuie Seale.
The Lord Admirall.
The Duke of Lenox.
The Marquesse of Buckinghame.
The Lord Chamberlaine.
The Earle of Arundell.
The Earle of South-hampton.
The Earle of Hertford.
The Earle of Essex
The Earle of Dorset.
The Earle of Mountgomerie.
The Viscount Lisle.
The Viscount Wallingford.
The Bishop of London.
The Bishop of Winchester.
The Bishop of Ely.
The Lord Zouch.
The Lord Windsor.
The Lord Wentworth.
The Lord Darcie.
The Lord Wootton.
The Lord Stanhope.
The Lord Carew.
The Lord Hay.
The Lord Chiefe Iustice of the Kings-Bench.
The Lord Chiefe Iustice of the Common-Pleas.
The Lord Chiefe Baron of the Excheaquer.

FINIS.

TO THOSE NOBLE
Personages rancked in the
CATALOGVE.

MY feebler Muse farre too too weake to sing,
 Ha's got your Honours on her flaggring wing,
And borne them to the loftiest pitch she may.
Therefore (submissiue) she do's humbly pray,
That when her tongue reeles, or Inuention haults,
Your Fauours will giue crutches to her faults.

Your Lordships in

all dutifull *obseruancie,*

H. G.

To The King.

THose (mighty Soueraigne) are your Graces text,
  Right King of Heralds, not to any, next:
You might their mysticke learning blazon best,
But you reserue your knowledge vnexprest:
As being most peculiar to you:
And yet because the people may allow
That which concernes your selfe: Let me to them
Vnlocke the value of this prizelesse Iem:
The *Lyons trebled* thus, may represent
Your equall fitnes for the Regiment
Of this faire Monarchie: *Brittaine* then
Which euer ha's bin stuft with valiant men,
May fittest beare a Lyon, vrg'd to spoile:
Your *Irish* Kernes, who neuer vs'd to toyle,
Are in their *siluer-studded Harpe* explain'd.
These *Splendent Beauties* limm'd by Natures hand,
  By grace of Ancient Kings, made Royall *flow'rs*,
  But now thrice Royall made, by being Yours.

B

EMBLEME I

WHy be these marshal'd equall, as you see?
    Are they dif-rankt, or not? No: they should be
Thus plac'd: for Common-weales doe tottering stand,
Not vnder-propt thus by the mutuall hand
Of *King* and *Priest*, by Gods and humane lawes:
Divine assistance most effectuall drawes
Kings to confesse, that t'heav'n they homage owe;
Which consequently leads a King to knowe,
That, that *Ambition's* by dead Embers fir'd,
Which ha's no beyond earth to heav'n aspir'd:
Earth can but make a King of earth partaker,
But Knowledge makes him neerest like his maker.
For mans meere power not built on Wisdomes fort,
Do's rather pluck downe kingdomes than support.
Perfectly mixt, thus *Power* and *Knowledge* moue
About thy *iust* designes, ensphear'd with *loue*;
Which (as a glasse) serue neighbour-Kings, to see
How best to follow, though not equall thee.

EMBLEME 2

SEated on this *three-headed Mountaine high*,
Which represents *Great Brytaines Monarchie*,
Thus stand I furnisht t'entertaine the noise:
Of thronging clamours, with an equall poyse:
And thus addrest to giue a constant weight
To formall shewes, of *Vertue*, or *Deceit*:
Thus arm'd with *Pow'r* to punnish or protect,
When I haue weigh'd each scruple and defect:
Thus *plentifully* rich in parts and place
To giue *Aboundance*, or a poore disgrace:
But, how to make these in iust circle moue,
Heav'n crownes my head with *wisedome* from aboue.
Thus Merit on each part, to whom 'tis due,
With God-like power disbursed is by you.

TO THE QVEENE.

OF all proportions (Madam) diuers dare
Conclude that absolute, which is most square:
Well may they proue that Theoreme: for I know
Square Bodies doe the most perfection show:
Perfection still consisting in this best,
To stand more sure, the more it is suppreft.
Which speciall vertue chiefly doth belong
Vnto square bodies, or right do's them wrong:
Your Scutchion therefore, and the Honours due,
May constantly support your Worth and You;
Whose life's drawne out (vnsoild with subiects hate)
By such a Samplar, none can imitate.

EMBLEME 3.

Here aboue number, doth one *wonder* sit;
But *One,* yet in her owne, an infinit:
Being simply rare, no *Second* can she beare,
Two *Sunnes* were neuer seene stalke in one Spheare.
From old *Eliza's* Vrne, enricht with fire
Of glorious wonders, did your worth suspire:
So must, from your dead life-infusing flame,
Your *Multiplyed-selfe* rise thence the *Same*:
She whose faire Memories, by *Thespian* Swaines
Are sung, on *Rheins* greene banks, and flowrie plaines.
Thus Time alternates in its single turnes;
One *Phænix* borne, another *Phænix* burnes.
Your rare worths (matchlesse Queene) in you alone
Liue free, vnparalle'd, entirely *One.*

To The Prince.

Your Princedome's Enſigne here (Right-Royall Sir)
  May pinion your vp-ſoaring thoughts, and ſtirre
Them to a pitch of loftier eminence,
Then can be reached by baſe vulgar ſenſe.
Theſe *Plumes* (charact'red liuely ſignifie
Valour in warre, ioyn'd with *velocitie*.
The blacke Prince (bearing *Plumes*) approues this true,
When through the *French* he like *win'gd-lightning* flue,
And pull'd downe liues about him to the ground,
Till he himſelfe with death had circled round:
His very looke did threaten publicke death:
With every ſtroke fell from him, fled a breath.
Arm'd in the confidence of his iuſt cauſe,
Thus freely feareleſſe his foes overthrowes.
Thoſe high-borne acts which from his valour flue,
  With new-additions are impreſs't in you.

EMBLEME 4

WHen *Peace* (suspecting he would *warre* inferre,)
 Tooke *Henry* hence, to liue aboue with her,
She bade *Ioues Bird* returne from's quicke convoy
Of *his faire* soule, left in Heav'ns lasting Ioy,
And mildly offer to your Princely hands,
This *Embleme* of soft *Peace* and *warlike bands*:
Both which (vs'd rightly) their *large cares* extend
To gaine o're *others*, and their *owne* defend.
Though all bright *Honours* did their Beauties shroud
In his *Ecclipse*, like *Phœbus* in a cloud:
Yet at your Rising, they more cleare againe
Peept-forth, like Sun-shine after clouds and raine.
And in your *worth* their worthinesse displayes
To worthiest Princes; as the Sun his rayes.

TO THE ARCH-BISHOP OF CANTERBVRY.

HOw well these sacred *Ornaments* become
One, who by earth walkes t'his celestiall home:
The *Staffe* of Comfort this, to leane vpon,
This, *Pall* of peace; these, *Crosses* vndergone:
How easily good men (knowne well by this)
Lodge at the Inne of their eternall Blisse:
These *Fruits*, are workes, from *Bounty* springing found,
Perfuming Heau'n, & with Heau'ns bounties crown'd:
These shadow'd fruits, but by a figure, shew
The Ioyes of *Paradise* prepar'd for you:
Saile thither with good speede then, yet make stay;
Good Angels guide you, y'are i'th Abbots way.

EMBLEMES.

THese *Hands* connext, engird *Religion*,
  Deciphring th'holy *Concords* vnison,
Of faiths full harmony: this *spiny pale*
Sharpe conflicts are, who still the *Truth* assaile:
This *Heart* the *Church* is, th'holy *Ghost* being *Center*,
Afflictions may surround, but cannot enter.
You are the prime linke of this *manuall chaine*,
Whereby *Religion* do's its strength maintaine:
O! may the *Reuerend Rest* to you sticke fast,
That *Truth* (though long) yet conquer may at last.

To The Lord Chancellor.

THe *North* and *Southerne Poles*, the two fix'd Starres
Of worth and dignitie, which all iust warres,
Should still maintaine, together: be here met
And in your selfe as in your Scutchion set:
The *halfe Moone* 'twixt, threatens as yet no change,
Or if she doe, she promises to range,
Till she againe recouer what she lost:
Your endlesse fame, (so) gaines your *Bounties* cost.

EMBLEME 6.

NEuer should any thinke himselfe so sure
Of friends assistance, that he dares procure
New enemies: for vnprouok'd they will
Spring out of forg'd, or causelesse malice still.
Else, why should this poore creature be pursu'd,
Too simple to offend, a beast so rude.
Therefore prouide (for malice danger brings)
House-roome to find vnder an *Eagles* wings.
You are this *Eagle*, whcih ore-shades the *sheepe*
Pursu'de by *humane wolues*, and safe doth keepe
The poore mans honest, though might-wronged cause,
From being crushed by oppressions pawes.
Faire Port you are, where euery *Goodnesse* findes
Safe shelter from swolne *Greatnesse*, stubborne winds
Eager to drench it: but that feareleffe rest
Dwels in your harbour, to all good distrest.
I bid not you prouide, you are compleate,
The good for to protect, or bad defeate.

TO THE LORD TREASVRER.

YOur *sable Crescent* might to some (whose lips
  Speake ignorance) portend a blacke Ecclipse:
I rather thus discerne, how Time would shroud
Your radiant *Crescent* in a *sable* Cloud:
And hold those enuious, ignorant, or dull,
That cannot see, your *Crescent* growing full.

EMBLEME 7.

The carefull *States-man*, who the *Key* doth carie
Of a a Kings *Treasury*, must not (partiall) varie:
But to iust causes compasse still be ti'de:
For *Iustice* (vniust shutting) opens wide,
And lets in hard *Opinion*, to disgrace
His *Soueraignes selfe*, his *Person*, and his *place*.
Nor must he carelesse slumber: but thus keepe
His lids vnshut-vp by soft-fingred *Sleepe*:
And hold a Counsell with the saddest howres
Of silent Night: and spend his purest powers
In care, to render to whom dues belong,
That *Subiects* may haue right, and *Kings* no wrong.
But you (Great Lord) beare vp this waight of *Trust*.
With a most *easie* Care, because most *iust*.

TO THE LORD PRIVY SEALE.

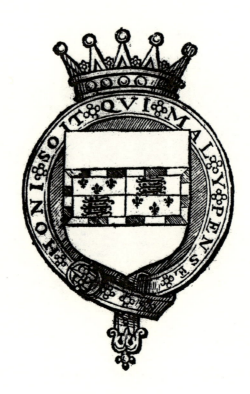

THose *dressings* that adorne *both parts* of Nature,
 First, is exprest in this *Maiesticke Creature*:
Next, in these *Flowres of Light* both which present
Your *Honours* at full height of complement,
And *Clearnesse*, which runnes through your *noble Blood*.
Mixt with this two-fold tincture, *Great* and *Good*:
What's here but shadow'd then, by *outward kind*,
Bedeckes the *inner Roomes* of your braue *mind*.

EMBLEME 12.

WHen ere thou draw'ſt out thy reuenging rod,
Let be for *Countrey*, and the *cauſe* of *God*:
Elſe thy *Oblations* will thy curſes be,
When thou encountreſt with thine enemy.
Nor is it ſacrifice that can appeaſe
Gods wrath, vnleſſe the mans obedience pleaſe
More then his offering : for if his dull heart
Thinkes he inricheth God in any part,
By offering *Hecatombs*, he looſeth all :
Nay further yet, he giues a *ſword* with all
To Heau'ns high Iuſtice, by inuoking downe
Reuenge, in lieu of *Guerdon*, or a *Crowne*.
Such as were ſacrifices once, ſuch bee
Our prayers ſtill, and our true *Sanctitie* :
Which is your In-mate and familiar gueſt,
More clearely ſeene in You, then here expreſt.

To The Lord Admirale.

YOur *sable mullet* like a *Starre* in *blacke*,
Shewes what our honour'd Admirall doth lacke:
And shewes as if that Starre of *Effingham*,
Were thus bemourn'd in a briefe *Epigram*:
This may your *Pole-starre* be, most noble Lord,
And guide you vnto that (so much abhorr'd)
The mournfull, yet the blessed, Port of death,
Blowne by the prayers of all good mens breath.

EMBLEME 9.

QVEL CHE DRITTO DA IL CIEL ✚ TORCER NON PVOSSI ✚

SVppose a *Globe* were fast'ned in the skie,
With cordes depending on it quarterly,
And men should striue by violence to wrest
That cordage to what crooked forme they list,
All wise men would conceiue them madly bent,
Why should they else impossibles attempt?
And we may thinke it as absurd a drift
In him, who craftily shall hope to shift
When *Fate* forbids him, or shall hope to thwart
The good intentions of an honest heart.
For that which heau'n directs (all ages see)
May iniured, but not diuerted be.
Seeke then no further, honest meanings can
Make a *plaine minde* best *policy* in man.

D

To The Dvke Of Lenox.

VVHat neede I further striue to amplifie
    Your high-borne worths, and noble dignitie:
Then by these *beautious flowres*, which declare;
Your mind's faire puritie, vnstain'd, and bare:
These golden *Buckles* bordring them about,
A Palizado, to keepe Foulenesse out.

EMBLEME 10.

THe *wolfe* and *Lyon* once together met,
And by agreement they their purpose set
To hunt together: when they had obtainde
Their bootie long pursude, the *wolfe* refrainde
No more then formerly, from greedinesse:
The *Lyon* apprehending, that much lesse
Might satisfie a beast no bigger growne,
Thought all the purchase rather was his owne:
And thought suppression of a beast so base
Was *Iustice*, to preserue the common race
Of harmlesse beasts; then speedily he teares
The *wolfe*, to take away their vsuall feares:
Eu'n thus when our great *Monarch* clearely saw,
How that insatiate *wolfe* of *Rome* did draw
More riches to his coffers, then deare soules
To Heau'n, he like this *Lyon* then controules
His vsurpation, deeming him a slaue,
Who more intended to deuoure, then saue.
But you know best to follow, in free course,
The Best in best things, and passe by the worse.

To The Marqvesse Of Bvckingham.

ALL that we see is comely, and delights
The eyes; which still are pleas'd with pretious
And (as your golden *Scallops*) You appeare   (sights:
To promise (that which we may value deare)
More then a glorious out-side, which containes
Meate, not to be disclos'd without due paines;
Thus is it scarce to be imagin'd how
Desert should paralell your worth, or You.

EMBLEME II.

THis glorious *Starre* attending on the *Sunne*,
Having, from this low world, iust wonder wonne
For brightnes; *Envie*, that foule *Stygian* brand,
T' extinguish it thrusts forth her greedie *hand*:
To catch it from its mounted moving place,
And hurle it lower to obscur'd *Disgrace*:
But while she snatches, to put out the flame,
Foolishly *fiers* her *fingers* with the same.
Who others glories striue t' eclipse (poore Elues)
Doe but drawe downe selfe-mischiefe on themselues.
You waiting on the *Sunne* of *Maiestie*
May that *elamping Heliotropium* be:
Still bright in your *Eclipticke* circle runne,
Y' are out of *Envies* reach, so neare the *Sunne*.
Moue fairely, freely in your wonted *Orbe*,
Aboue the danger of *Detractions* curbe,
And her selfe-bursting Brood: sit there, contemne,
Nay laugh, and scorne both their despight, and them.

To The Lord Chamberline.

NOt becaufe you are given to rage or fpoile,
Like *rampant Lyons*e, which deferue a Toyle:
Nor yet becaufe your gifts devided be,
Do Lyons thus divide themfelues in three:
But (when provok'd) to fhew you can refift,
Or fhew your courage when Your Honor lift:
Or thus in number they doe looke one way,
To fhew, what You command, your friends obey.

EMBLEME 12.

Fixt heere snow-vested *Pietie* remaines
Al-pure, and in all pure, purg'd from the staines
Of all false worship, chaste as aire, vntainted
With the foule blemishes of that al-painted
Proude Curtizan: nor wander do's her mind,
Shee best content in *Constancy* doth find:
To *Alethea's* pillar close she clings,
Maugre the rapting straines *Romes* Syren sings:
Who is athirst, and do's but touch her *Cup*,
Drinkes, with delight, his soule's saluation vp.
Thus comprehends she ioyes, which most would buy
At the high'st rate, in this one *Constancy*,
So aboue others may your *Honour* shine,
As past all others, do's this *Forme Diuine*,
With her ingenuous Beames blaze bright in you,
Who's doubly gilt, with *Her*, and *Learning* too.

To The Earle Of Arvndell.

ON *Gules* you beare the figure of a *Bend*
Betweene *croſſe croſſelets* fixt: which all intend
Rightly to ſhadow *Noble birth*, adorn'd
With valour, and a Chriſtian cauſe, not ſcorn'd
By any but by Infidels, and they
Miſtaking this, their hel-bred hate diſplay.
But to leaue ſhadowes, you (ſubſtantiall) ſhine
With thoſe good things, which make a man diuine.

EMBLEME 13.

KNow (honour'd Sir) that th'heate of *Princes* loue,
Throw'n on those reall *worths*, good men approue
Doth, like the radiant *Phœbus* shining here,
Make fruitfull vertue at full height appeare:
T'illustrate this in you, were to confesse
How much your *Goodnesse* doth your *Greatnesse* blesse,
By its owne warme reflexe: Thus both suruiue,
And both i'th *Sunne* of *Royall fauour* thriue.
O may's reuerberating rayes still nourish
Your noble *worths*, and make your *Vertues* flourish.

E

To The Earle Of Sovth-hampton.

NO storme of troubles, or cold frosts of Friends,
Which on free *Greatnes*, too too oft, attends,
Can (by presumption) threaten your free state:
For these presaging *sea-birds* doe amate
Presumptuous *Greatnes*: mouing the best mindes,
By their approach, to feare the future windes
Of all calamitie, no lesse then they
Portend to sea-men a tempestuous day:
Which you foreseeing may before hand crosse,
As they doe them, and so prevent the losse.

27.

EMBLEME 13.

VVHat coward *Stoicke*, or blunt captaine will
Dis-like this *Vnion*, or not labour still
To reconcile the *Arts* and *victory*?
Since in themselues Arts haue this quality,
To vanquish errours traine: what other than
Should loue the Arts, if not a valiant man?
Or, how can he resolue to execute,
That hath not first learn'd to be resolute?
If any shall oppose this, or dispute,
Your great example shall their spite confute.

E 2

28.

To The Earle Of Hertford:

THese Lyons gardant wisely seeme to take
  The name of gardant, for the flowers sake:
As if they kept the flower-de-luces thus
From them, who any way obnoxious,
Might gather them: it is a noble part,
To keepe the glories purchas'd by desert.

EMBLEME 12.

THis *Triple Cloſe*, if diſ-united, none:
But knit by faith, an indiuiduall *One*.
Standing vnmoou'd like an heroicke rocke,
Affronts the batt'ries of fierce *Enuies* ſhocke.
God, Heart, Religion, theſe, *One*, made of *three*,
Ioyn'd in vnſeuer'd threefold *Vnitie*,
Royall paire-royall (ſee) three are the ſame,
He that hath this paire-royall wins the game.
View, how this heart, and how theſe hands agree,
Whoſe heart, and hands are one, thrice happy hee.
And though two hands, yet but one are theſe two,
Both doe the ſame, and both the ſame vndoe.
Concord makes in a million, but one heart,
Whereat ſterne *Hate* may leuell her fierce dart,
And deepely wound too, yet cannot that wound
Diſanimate, or her free thoughts confound:
But with a double *Valour* ſhe vp-beares
Such hearts, aboue the ſtroke of baſer feares.
Thus you within haue rais'd vp ſuch a fort,
As keepes out Ills, and doth your good ſupport.

To The Earle Of Essex.

The chiefest of this Scuchion comprehends
Three *Torteaux*, which vnto all commends
A firme and plenteous liberality,
Proper to you, and to your familie:
And this one vertue, in you (cleare as day)
All other vertues elements display.

31.

EMBLEME 16.

NO wild, or desperate foole can hence collect
Proofe to applaud his vice, or to protect:
Nor can this *Figure* civill warre portend,
Whither oppose, or whither it defend:
But auntient *Valour*, that which hath advanc'd
Our *Predeceſſours*, (while fine Courtiers danc'd)
That's heere infer'd, to re-informe the mind
By view of instances, wherein we find
Recorded of your Auncestrie, whose fame
Like forked thunder, threaten'd cowards shame;
Who fearing, lest on their deboſh'd baſe merit,
Heav'n should drop Bolts, by a flame-winged spirit.

To The Earle Of Dorset.

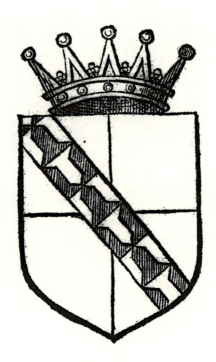

T'Is true, your various *Bend* thus quarterly
  Describ'd, poynts out the great antiquitie,
Of *Honour*, and of *Vertue* truely claim'd
By You, who haue preseru'd them free, vnmaim'd.
Let none that's generous thinke his time ill spent,
To imitate your *worths* so eminent.

33.

EMBLEME 17.

THe *world* whose happinesse, and cheife delight,
Nay more, whose *wisedome* lies in *Appitite*,
Rather then *Knowledge*; claimes the largest share
Of that which pleaseth most: nor doth it care
To comprehend a higher mysterie:
And therefore well doth nature dignifie
Th' ascending point, with heau'ns neere neighbour (hood
Leauing to earth what's *great*, to heau'n what's *good*.
   Which you perceiuing, wisely doe bestow, low.
   Your thoughts on Heav'n, your wealth on things be-
F

To The Earle Of Movntgomery.

The *Crescent* to a second House belongs,
  The golden *Crescent* (worth a Poets songs)
Well appertaines vnto thy *House* and *thee*,
Thou Arch-supporter of *Mountgomery*.
For not the vaprous breath of bad report,
Can cloud the splendour thou deseru'st in Court:
But as in gold no rust can finde a place,
So hath thy *Crescent* no enforc'd disgrace.

EMBLEME 18.

AS busie Bees vnto their Hiue doe swarme,
So do's th'attractiue power of *Musicke* charme
All *Eares* with silent rapture: nay, it can
Wilde *Reason* re-contract, diuorc'd from man.
Birds in their warblings imitate the *Spheares*:
This sings the *Treble*, that the *Tenour* beares:
Beasts haue with listning to a Shepheards lay,
Forgot to feed, and so haue pin'd away:
Brookes that creepe through each flowr-befretted field,
In their harmonious murmurs, musicke yeeld:
Yea, senselesse *stones* at the old *Poets* song,
Themselues in heapes did so together throng,
That to high beauteous structures they did swell
Without the helpe of *hand*, or vse of *skill*:
This *Harmony* in t'humane *Fabricke* stealesː
And is the sinewes of all Common-weales.
In you this *Concord's* so diuinely placed:
That *it* by *you*, not *you* by *it* is graced.

To The Lord Viscount Lisle.

Let there be no addition, this atone
Will make an *Embleme*, and a perfect one.
Conceiue it thus then: A *Darts forked head*
Apt to endanger, though not striking dead.
Such is, or should be every *noble mind*,
Prepar'd like this in most resolued kind
To wound, or kill offensiue iniury,
And though vnurg'd, yet threatens dangers nie.

EMBLEME 19.

Here *Sience* do's in contemplation sit,
Distinguishing by formes, the soule of wit:
Knowing, perfection ha's no proper grace,
If wanting *Order*, *Number*, *Time*, or *Place*:
The *Theoricke* and *Practicke* part must be
As heate and fire: the *Sunne*, and Claritie:
Such twins they are, and such Correlatiues,
As the'one without the other seldome thriues.
How can a man the feates of Armes well doe,
If not a *Scholler*, and a *Souldiour* too?
If either then be missing in's due place,
Defect steps in, and steales from all their grace:
On good acts you employ the *practicke* part,
The *Theory* lies lodg'd within your heart.

To The Lord Viscovnt Wallingford.

VVEll may you neuer find the want, or los.
Of that most hallowed, and instructing *Crosse*,
On which our *Saviour* di'de: for these will shew
The many blessed thoughts of that, in few:
Heere you may over-looke the world, and see
Nothing so plentifull, as crosses be:
Thence you may take occasion to prepare
Your soule, to beare those that worse crosses are.
These are the badges of Your noble brest,
That will conduct You to heave'ns quiet rest.

EMBLEME 20.

THus playes the Courtly *Sycophant*, and thus
Selfe-pleasing *Sinne*, which poysons all of vs:
Thus playd the whore whome the wise King describes
Thus he who rayles at, and yet pockets bribes:
Thus playes the *Polititian*, who will smile,
Yet like this Serpent sting your heart the while.
Bung vp thyne eares then, or suspect the harme,
When sweete *Cyllenian* words begin to charme.
But you, can these vnmask by knowing best
How to keepe such from lurking neere your breast.

To The Bishop Of London.

TWo swords there be, which all Diuines should take,
E're they this victory can perfect make;
Preuailing *Language* is a powerfull one,
Zeale for the truth, the other: these haue done
More noble acts, then warre could euer boast:
Both are in your Field found, though else-where lost.

41.

EMBLEME. 21.

ME thinkes (Right Reuerend) here you silence
Viewing this *Embleme*, & it thus bespeake:(breake,
Ride on Triumphing, make a glorious shew,
Catch those, who onely but thy *Out-side* know :
Hold forth thy witching *Cup*, aduance thy *Crowne*,
And'Mounted thinke thy selfe past pulling downe :
Yet after all, thou canst be prou'd no more,
Then a deluding, and deluded whore.

G

To The Bishop Of Winchester.

The *Sword* and *Keyes* to Church-men beene bequea-
Since *Paul* and *Peter* were of life bereaued: (thed,
The *Keyes*, a type of *Prayers*, which unlocke
Heau'ns glorious gates, to let in those that knocke.
The Spirits zealous, and soule-sauing *word*,
Is shadow'd by the sinne-subduing *Sword*:
Of *word* and *Sword* th'incorporate qualitie
Ha's power to heaue base earth aboue the skie.
Your powerfull, and victorious elegance,
Which ouercomes bold vice and arrogance,
Do's proue, no weapons to the Church belong,
But such as Heau'n makes to encounter wrong:
Nor do's your *Gentry* differ: *Lozenges*
Are curing Cordials: *Generous thoughts* like these.

EMBLEME 22.

Behold, on what the *Romaine Faith* consists:
So tost by *Errours* winds; so lapt in Mists:
That their *Arch-pilot* scarse can rule the sterne;
He lackes foundation, therefore still to learne
How to make's Ship his Harbour. O I wonder
Th'ore-burden'd Vessell crackes not quite asunder,
And sinkes not downe, opprest by its owne weight,
With sinfull soules so stuft, and over-freight.
The high *Auenger* (though he seemes to faile)
With winged wrath will split their proudest saile.
Heau'ns yron-hand (most slowly heau'd aloft)
Falls quicke, dead-sure, and home, although not oft
All wish, for their sakes of *Romes* simpler sort,
That you might steere their vessell to the Port:

To The Bishop Of Ely.

How much more better may you challenge thefe,
Then all your *Predeceſſors*, who in eaſe,
And floath (you being conſider'd) did neglect
That which deſerues a Crowne, or good reſpect:
Theſe then the Heralds may thinke rather due,
Not to your place of ſtate, but vnto you.

EMBLEME 23.

REligion still its owne, cannot be lost,
Nor from it selfe diuorc'd, though to the most,
Who iudge by guesse and slight formality,
There might appeare schisme in *Diuinity*:
When not *Diuinity*, which cannot change,
But humane *reason* to schismes vild doth range:
For so the fruites of diuers plants may seeme
Diuers in quality: and men may deeme
Nature hath err'd in such a serious course,
When both consider'd be the same in force.
You, that best iudge of Schismes, can clearely see,
Error term'd *Truth*, and *Truth* term'd Heresie.

To The Lord Zovch

SEe, how a *worthy spirit* not imployde
May seeme to lookers on, or vaine, or voyd:
These *golden peeces* thus vnshap't, vncoin'd,
Seeme as if *worth* and they were quite disioyn'd:
When brasse or copper being stamp't or fram'd
Into the shape of plate, is oft misnam'd,
And oft mistaken for the purest gold:
But you are euer actiue, and vnfold
Your pretious substance, that your selfe may take,
Honours true stampe; what's counterfeite forsake.

EMBLEME 24.

HEere *Phœbus* and the Sacred *Sisters* sit,
Chiefely attending *Harmonie*, and *wit*:
Who stay to heare the dying Swans to sing
Sad *Epods*; riding on the *Thespian* Spring.
Heere the *wing'd-Horses* hoofe digs vp that *well*
Whence gurgle streames of *Art*, and sacred *Skill*.
Divines (like *Pegasus*) divinely mooue
In Man, springs of profound, and precious loue
To heav'nly *wisedome*; who t'ech passing by,
Poynts out the path-way to *Eternitie*.
And whilst You doe your noble thoughts confine
To what *Divines* preach, You become Divine.

TO THE LORD WINDSOR.

ME thinkes, I see in this, the true estate
Of man still subiect to a lucklesse fate:
As if the greatest *Crosse* did represent
The generall curse, which even all over went.
From Adam to his wretched progeny:
The lesser *Crosses* which accompany
The greater, be each severall haplesse chance:
And all together shew, that ignorance
Is irrecoverably blind, where none
Prevents what happens thus to every one.
But You doe well support the waightiest crosses
With Patience, and esteeme them but light losses.

EMBLEME 25.

YEe, whose blind folly doth not so maintaine
A former choice, but yee may chuse againe:
And yee, whose innocence (not knowing yet
The worse from better) carelesly doth let
Both rest vnchosen; now begin to make
Your new, or first choise, and heere wisely take
The patterne: if you would encline to Peace,
Loue bookes with *Vertue* stor'd, so will decrease
Your troubles: those will bring such powerfull fame
As shall the sternest Lyon soonest tame.
Experience leades thee to this certaine choice.
Chuse then at first, to grieue, or to reioice.
You haue already chosen true *Content*:
Nor needs your Honour euer to repent.

H.

To The Lord Wentvvorth.

L*Eopards* haue euer ranked bin among
Those nobler beasts, which are both swift & strong.
Swiftnes alludes to a dexteritie;
Or quicke dispatch without temeritie.
Their *strength* alludes to *Iudgement* which indures,
When flashing *wit* no long delight assures.
Make these your owne, and then you beare display'd,
Your Scutchions morrall, in your selfe pourtray'd.

EMBLEME 26.

IOue, *Phœbus*, and *Minerua* were assign'd,
To be the three chiefe ornaments of mind.
Ioue figur'd *Prouidence*, *Minerua*, *Wit*,
Phœbus, *Content*: and all that purchas'd it
Well are they seated in a holy place,
To shew the Continent of all, is grace:
It seemes that yon haue well consider'd thus:
The fair'st of titles is, *Religious*.

H 2

To The Lord Darcie.

These health-preseruing *leaues* thus inly fixt
   Amongst the *Crosselets*, shew, heau'ns fauours mixt
With all calamities that seaze on man,
If patiently he entertaine them can.
To find cure then for Crosses, looke aboue.
See, ill made well by heau'ns all-curing loue.

EMBLEME 27.

Sleepe, being the type of death: darknesse must be
The shade of that, which we euanisht see:
Men so departed, that it may be said,
A *Bird*, as well, as such a man, is dead:
Chase, while thou liu'it, the cloudes of death away:
Or dying, neuer looke to see more day.
You haue on earth, so studied heau'ns delight,
That you can neuer be obscur'd: though night
Should threaten to obscure noone-day, yet will
Your *Noble-mind* vanquish *deaths* darkest ill.

To The Lord Wotton.

Setled afflictions may be well expres't
 Vnder this forme of *Crosses*, which men blest
Haue still indur'd to proue their patience :
But I would rather in another sence
Haue this appli'de to such a man, whose vowes
Haue fixt him to the faith *Christs* Church allowes :
And such a man (scorning vngrounded wrongs)
Are you, to whom this fixed *Crosse* belongs.

EMBLEME 28.

TH'ascending Path that vp to wisedome leades
Is rough, vneuen, steepe: and he that treades
Therein, must many a tedious *Danger* meet,
That, or trips vp, or clogs his wearied feet:
Yet led by *Labour*, and a quicke *Desire*
Of fairest *Ends* scrambles, and clambers higher
Then *Common reach*: still catching to holde fast
On strong'st *Occasion*, till he come at last
Vp to *Her* gate, where *Learning* keepes the key,
And lets him in, *Her* best Things to suruay:
There he vnkend (though to himselfe best knowne)
Takes rest, till Time presents him with a Crowne:
In quest of this rich Prize, your toyle's thus graced:
Euer to be in Times best Border placed.

To The Lord Stanhope.

This enterchang'd variety of *Furre*,
   And naked quarters, fitly doe concurre.
To shew the seasonable contenting storc
That rich wise men in ioy, alike with poore:
Both are prouided (lest they might take harme)
To keepe their innocence, both safe and warme.

EMBLEME 29.

IMagine heere, *Christ* strongly fortifi'd,
Against the *Popes* bold heresie and pride:
And thinke, whilst his Accomplices combine
The Castle of *Christs* truth, to vndermine;
A flame breakes forth, which doth consume them all:
So seeking his, they meete with their owne fall.
And thus whilst heretickes (like wretched elues)
Out-stare the *Truth*, they doe condemne themselues,
Subiected to the twofold victory
Of *Truth*, and of their owne impietie.
Take refuge then, in Heau'ns eternall rest,
And see Christs foes against themselues addrest.

I

To The Lord Carevv.

The noblest parts of *wisedome*, as *cleare wit*,
High *Courage*, and such vertues kinne to it:
Should ever be proceeding, and goe on
Forward, as seeme these *Lyons*, vrg'd of none.
So (like to these) You keepe a passant pace,
Till *wisedome* seate You in your wished place.

EMBLEME. 30.

FOrces vnited geminate their force,
And so doth vertue: never should remorse
Nor obstacle restraine that man, who may
Strengthen his vertues by a noble way:
Who cannot perfect be, needes not repent
To add his owne t' anothers President.
And he that is entire may therewithall,
By others helpe proue more effectuall.
So helpe me Learning, as I doe not know,
Where I this *Embleme* fitter may bestowe.

60.

To The Lord Hayes.

BEauties chiefe elements of *white* and *Red*
Is all that in your *Coate* is figured:
Nor is it needfull, any thing should be
Added to this most copious mysterie:
Gules vpon *Argent* to conceit are playne,
And pourtray out a life without all staine.

EMBLEME 31.

SEe *Bountie* seated in her best of pride,
Whose fountaines never ebbe, ever full tide
At every change : see; from her streaming heart,
How rivulets of *Comfort* doe impart
To *worth* dryde vp by *want*; and to asswage
The drought of *Vertue* in her pilgrimage.
Looke, how her wide-stretcht, fruit-befurnisht hand
Vnlockt to true *Desert*, do's open stand:
But if she should not be *Deserts* regarder,
Yet is it, in it selfe, its owne rewarder.
This *Emblem's* not presented (Noble Sir)
Your bounteous nature to awake, or stir :
For you are *Bounties Almner*, and do's know,
How to refraine, destribute, or bestow.

TO THE THREE LORDS CHIEFE IVSTICES.

BY these life-lengthning *Lozenges*, are show'n
Cares to cure *Ills*, by times corruption grow'n.
To comfort *Vertues* heart, at point to die
Of a Consumption, and doth bed-rid lie:
This *Starre*, that *Iustice* is, which is not blind,
(As th'ancient Hieroglyphickes her defin'd)
But searcheth out with quicke discerning eye
Th'hard difference twixt *Faith* and *Fallacy*.
These *Birds*, as yet vnlearnt to light on earth,
Figure that *Iustice*, which from Heau'n ha's Birth,
And scornes to looke so low, as base *respect*
Of its owne priuate *ends*, and *Truth* neglect.
Care, *Truth*, and *Iustice* thus vnite, we see
Make in their *Goodnesse* mixt, a Sympathy,
On whose ioynt pinions th' Realmes *Peace* vp-towres
T'her Chaire of State, subsisteted by your powres.

EMBLEME 32.

SHe that illuminates the midnight, may
Be well admitted to take rest all day:
Yet haue our antique Poets rather made
Night-wandring *Luna* t'haue a daily Trade;
Reporting, that by day she takes delight
To hunt wilde creatures, and then shines at night:
Teaching (or I mistake) how *Magistrates*
Should quell *Disorders* in all ciuill States.
In darknesse they should watchfull insight keepe,
To hunt out *Vice*, when men are thought asleepe:
For *Mischiefe* (as in darknesse) skulkes disguis'd,
And therefore needs some watchfully aduis'd,
Who hauing sented out this secret game,
May then pursue them to a publicke shame.
But your deepe wisedomes, better know, then this,
What in our *Common-weale* most needfull is.

MINERVA BRITANNA

OR A GARDEN OF HEROICAL
Deuises, furnished, and adorned with *Emblemes* and *Impresa's* of sundry natures, Newly devised, moralized, and published,

By HENRY PEACHAM, Mr. of Artes.

LONDON
Printed in Shoe-lane at the signe of the Faulcon by Wa: Dight.

Plate 2. *Nisi desuper.*

To my dread Soveraigne IAMES, *King of great* BRITAINE. *&c.*

<small>Tibi serviet
ultima Thvle,
Virgil:
THVLEM
procul Axe re-
motam.
Claudian.
Schetland.
et nautis nostris
hodie Thilensel.</small>

A SECRET arme out stretched from the skie,
  In double chaine a Diadem doth hold:
Whose circlet boundes, the greater BRITANNIE,
From conquered FRAVNCE, to * THVLE sung of old:
Great IAMES, whose name beyond the INDE is told:
  To GOD obliged so by two-fold band,
  As borne a man, and Monarch of this land.

<small>Διοτρεφέας
βασιλῆας.
Homer.</small>

Thus since on heauen, thou wholly dost depend:
  And from * aboue thy Crowne, and being hast:
With malice vile, in vaine doth man intend,
T'vnloose the knot that GOD hath link't so fast:
Who shoot's at * heauen, the arrow downe at last
  Lightes on his head: and vengeance fall on them,
  That make their marke, the Soveraigne Diadem.

<small>Basil: Doron.
lib. 1. pag. 2.</small>   Nubibus en duplici vinctum Diadema catena,
    Quod procul a nostro sustinet orbe manus:
   Non alia te lege Deus (IACOBE) ligavit,
    Quem regere imperio, fecit, et esse virum.

Sic pacem habemus.

To the High and mightie *IAMES*, King of greate Britaine,

TWOO Lions stout the Diadem vphold,
  Of famous Britaine, in their armed pawes:
The one is Red, the other is of Gold,
And one their Prince, their sea, their land and lawes;
  Their loue, their league: whereby they still agree,
  In concord firme, and friendly amitie.

Scilicet Anglicus et Scoticus.

BELLONA henceforth bounde in Iron bandes,
Shall kisse the foote of mild triumphant PEACE,
Nor Trumpets sterne, be heard within their landes;
Envie shall pine, and all old grudges cease:
  Braue Lions, since, your quarrell's lai'd aside,
  On common foe, let now your force be tri'de.

Vnum sustentant gemini diadema Leones,
  Concordes vno Principe, mente, fide.

Fœdere iunguntur simili, cœloque, saloque,
  Nata quibus Pax hæc inviolanda manet.

Plate 4 31 *Protegere Regium.*

WHILE deadly foes, their engines haue prepard;
    with furie fierce, to batter downe the walles,
My dutie is the Citie gate to guard,
And to rebate their Rammes, and fierie balls:
    So that if firmely, I do stand without,
    Within the other, neede no daunger doubt.

Dread Soveraigne *IAMES*, whose puissant name to heare,
The Turke may tremble, and the Traitor pine:
Belou'd of all thy people, farre and neere:
Bee thou, as this Port-cullies, vnto thine,
    Defend without, and thou within shalt see,
    A thousand thousand, liue and die with thee.

> Obsessis ut opem certo numine præstem,
> Quæ non sustineo damna creata mihi.
> Sis cataracta tuis (animose Monarcha) Britannis,
> Intus et invenies pectora firma tibi.

Si status Imperii, aut salus provinciarum
in discrimen vertatur, debebit (Princeps) in acie stare.   *Tacit* 4 *Hist.*

Hibernia Respub: ad Iacobum Regem.

WHILE I lay bathed in my natiue blood,
 And yeelded nought saue harsh, & hellish soundes:
And saue from Heauen, I had no hope of good,
Thou pittiedst (Dread Soveraigne) my woundes,
 Repair'dst my ruine, and with Ivorie key,
 Didst tune my strings, that slackt or broken lay.

Now since I breathed by thy Roiall hand,
And found my concord, by so smooth a tuch,
I giue the world abroade to vnderstand,
Ne're was the musick of old Orpheus such,
 As that I make, by meane (Deare Lord) of thee,
 From discord drawne, to sweetest vnitie.

Cum mea nativo squallerent sceptra cruore,
 Edoque lugubres vndique fracta modos:
Ipse redux nervos distendis (Phœbe) rebelles,
 Et stupet ad nostros Orpheus ipse sonos.

Ex vtroque Immortalitas.

Ad pijssimum Iacobum magnæ Britanniæ Regem.

Bonus Princeps nihilo differt a bono patre.

* *Hanc animam interea cæso de corpore raptam Fac iubar vt semper Capitolia nostra forumque Divus ab excelsa prospectet Iulius æde. Ovid: Metamor: 15.*

* *Pietate, et Iustitia, Principes Dij fiunt. Augustus dictum apud Senecam in Ludo.*

BVt thou whose goodnes, Pietie, and Zeale,
   Haue caus'd thee so, to be belou'd of thine,
(When envious Fates, shall robbe the Common weale,
Of such a * Father,) shalt for ever shine:
   Not turn'd as * *Cæsar*, to a fained starre,
   But plac'd a * Saint, in greater glory farre.

With whome mild *Peace*, the most of all desir'd;
And learned Muse shall end their happie dayes;
While thou to all eternitie admir'd,
Shalt liue afresh, in after ages praise:
   Or be the Loade-starre, of thy glorious North,
   Drawing all eies, to wonder at thy worth.

Ex Basil: nostr.

    Te tua sed Pietas omni memorabilis ævo,
      Sidus ad æterni Cæsaris vsque feret:
    Iustitia occumbet tecum, quia Musa, Fidesque
      In patriam, raris pax et habenda locis.

13 **TO THE THRICE-VERTVOVS, AND FAIREST OF QVEENES, ANNE QVEENE OF GREAT BRITAINE.**

Anagramma D:
Gul: Fouleri.

In ANNA regnantium arbor.
ANNA *Britannorum Regina*.

AN Oliue lo, with braunches faire difpred,
 Whofe top doth feeme to peirce the azure skie,
Much feeming to difdaine, with loftie head
The Cedar, and thofe Pines of THESSALIE,
 Faireft of Queenes, thou art thy felfe the Tree,
 The fruite * thy children, hopefull Princes three.

* Non claffes, non Legiones, &c. de firma imperii munimenta quam numerum liberorum. Tacitus. 4. Hift:

* parcere fubiect- &c.

Which thus I gheffe, fhall with their outftretcht armes,
 In time o'refpread Europa's continent,
* To fhield and fhade, the innocent from harmes,
 But overtop the proud and infolent:
  Remaining, raigning, in their glories greene,
  While man on earth, or Moone in heauen is

E corpore pulchro Gratior.

TO THE RIGHT NOBLE, AND MOST TOWARDLY YOVNG PRINCE, *CHARLES* DVKE OF *YORKE.*

SWEETE Duke, that bear'st thy Fathers Image right
Aswell in * bodie, as thy towardly mind;
Within whose cheeke * me thinkes in Red and white
Appeare the Roses yet againe conioind;
   Where, howsoe're their warres appeased be,
   Each, striues with each, for Soueraignitie.

Since Nature then in her faire-Angell mould,
Hath framd thy bodie, shew'd her best of art:
Oh let thy mind the * fairest virtues hold,
Which are the beautie of thy better part:
   And which,(braue CHARLES) shall make vs * lou'thee more,
   Then all thy state we outwardly adore.

videtur mihi
nus quæpiam
gratia conce
tari principe
Xenoph: in

* *Et diuitiae*
et formæ gl
fluxa atque f
lis est, virtus
ra æternaque
betur. Sal
Cat:

Ὡς ἡδὺ κάλ
ὁ ταῦ ἔχει τ
παφορά.
Menander.

Ex malis moribus bonæ leges.

To the most iudicious, and learned, Sir FRANCIS BACON, Knight.

THE Viper here, that stung the sheepheard swaine,
  (While careles of himselfe asleepe he lay,)
With Hysope caught, is cut by him in twaine,
  Her fat might take, the poison quite away,
    And heale his wound, that wonder tis to see,
    Such soveraigne helpe, should in a Serpent be.

By this same Leach, is meant the virtuous King,
Who can with cunning, out of manners ill,
Make wholesome lawes, * and take away the sting,
Wherewith foule vice, doth greeue the virtuous still:
  Or can prevent, by quicke and wise foresight,
  Infection ere, it gathers further might.

* vitiorum emendatricem legem esse oportet Cic
1 de legibus.

Salus Civitatis in legibus. Arist:

Afia venenato pupugit quem vipera morsu,
  Dux Gregis antidotum læsus ab hoste petit:
Vipereis itidem leges ex moribus aptas
  Doctus Apollinea conficit arte SOLON.

vitiis quæ plurima menti   Cura dedit leges et quod natura remittit.
Fœmineæ natura dedit humana malignas   Invida iura negat &c.

Ovid Metamor:
lib 10.

To the Right Honourable and my singuler good Lord HENRY
HOVVARD Earle of Northhampton, Lord Privie Seale. &c.

HENRICVS HOVVARDVS Comes Northamptoniensis.
Pius, Castus huic mentis honor, merè honorandus.

Anagramm
thoris.

A SNOW-WHITE Lion by an Altar sleepes,
(Whereon of Virtue are the Symboles plac't,)
Which day and night, full carefully he keepes,
Least that so sacred thing mought be defac't
 By Time, or Envie, who not farre away,
 Doe lurke to bring the same vnto decay.

Great Lord, by th' Altar Pietie is ment,
Thus, whereupon is virtue seated sure:
Which thou protectest with deare cherishment;
And dost thy best, their safetie to procure
 By howerly care, as doth this Lion white
 Tipe of thy mildnes, and thy feared might,

Distantia iungꝭ.

To the thrice Noble, and exellent Prince: *Ludowick* Duke of *Lennox*.

NOR may my Muse greate *Duke*, with prouder saile,
  Ore-passe your name, your birth, and best deserts:
But lowly strike, and to these cullors vaile,
That make ye yet belou'd in forrein partes,
In memorie of those disioined heartes:
    Of two great kingdomes, whom your grandsire wrought,
    Till Buckle-like, them both in one he brought.

* Mild *Peace* heerein, to make amendes againe,
Ordaines your daies ye shall dispend in rest,
While *Horror* bound, in hundred-double chaine,
At her faire feete, shall teare her snakie crest,
And *Mars* in vaine, with Trumpet sterne molest
    Our Muse, that shall her loftiest numbers frame,
    To eternize your *STEVVARTS* Roiall name.

* — Pax optima rerum
Quas homini nouisse datum est,
pax vna triúphis
Immeritis potior
Silius lib. 11.

Quod proauum virtus discordia iunxit in vnum   Cui LVDOVICE vices iterum PAX alma rependens,
Regna duo, hæc facto præmia digna tulit: Tempora dat rebus DIVA quieta tuis.   *Basil: Dorõ.*

Q 1.

Plate 12 21   *Gloria Principum.*

To the right truely Noble, and moſt Honourable Lord
VVILLIAM, *Earle of Penbrooke.*

Ta med : Adriani
Imp :

A LADIE faire, who with Maieſtique grace,
   Supportes a huge, and ſtately Pyramis.
(Such as th'old Monarches long agoe did place,
By NILVS bankes, to keepe their memories ;)
   Whoſe brow (with all the orient Pearles beſet,)
   Begirte's a rich and pretious Coronet.

Shee Glorie is of Princes, as I find
Deſcrib'd in Moneies, and in Meddailes old;
Thoſe Gemmes are glorious proiectes of the mind,
Adorning more their Roiall heades, then Gold.
   The Pyramis the worldes great wonderment,
   Is of their fame, ſome * laſting Moniment.

* Ingenii præ-
clara facinora ſi-
cut Anima Im-
mortalia ſunt.
Saluſt :

Ovid: ad L. ia.

      Facta Ducis vivent operoſaque gloria rerum
       Hæc manet hæc avidos effugit vna rogos.

His ornari aut mori.

To the right Honourable, and most noble Lord, HENRY, Earle of Southampton.

THREE Girlondes once, COLONNA did devize
   For his Impresa, each in other ioin'd;
The first of OLIVE, due vnto the wise,
The learned brow, the LAVRELL greene to bind:
   The OKEN was his due aboue the rest,
   Who had deserued in the Battaile best.

His meaning was, his mind he would apply
By due desert, to challenge each, his prize:
And rather choose a thousand times to die,
Then not be learned, valiant, and wise.
   How fewe alas, doe now adaies we finde
   (Great Lord) that beare, thy truely noble mind.

Ripa in
...

Plate 14 | *Psalmi Davidici.*

To the right Reverend Father in GOD, IOHN Bishop of London.

Basilic: Doron.
lib: 1. pag: 11.

* Liber omni'
Psalmorum simi
lis est vrbi pul-
chræ, atque mag-
næ, cui ædes co-
plures diverseque
sint, quarum fo-
res proprijs cla-
vibus diverseque
claudantur, quæ
cum in vnum lo-
cum cogestæ per-
mixtæque sint. &c
Hilar: in prolog :
psalmor explanat

TO sundry keies doth * HILARIE compare
   The holy Psalmes of that prophetique King,
Cause in their Natures so dispos'd they are,
That as it were, by sundry dores they bring,
   The soule of man, opprest with deadly sinne,
   Vnto the Throne, where he may mercy winne.

οἱ μὲν ἐν ὁμο-
μολῇ λεγόμενοι,
οἱ δὲ εν προςευ-
χῇ. οἱ δὲ εν
αινέσει. οἱ
δὲ ὡς ἐν εὐχῇ.
οἱ δὲ ὡς [εν]
ἐξομολογήσει.
Athanasius tomo
primo in Epist:ad
Marcellinum de
interpret: psal
mortu .

For wouldst thou in thy Saviour * still reioyce,
Or for thy sinnes, with teares lament and pray,
Or sing his praises with thy heart and voice,
Or for his mercies giue him thankes alway?
   Set DAVIDS Psalmes, a mirrour to thy mind,
   But with his Zeale, and heauenly spirit ioin'd.

Clavibus innexis hymnos HILARIVS æq tot,   Et vere, innumeros aditus hi quippe recludant
  Iessæ cecinit quos pia Musa senis,   Mens quibus ætherei pulsat Asyla DEI.

His altiora.

TO the honourable the Lord Wootton.

YEE Noblest sprightes, that with the bird of IOVE,
  Haue learnt to leaue, and loath, this baser earth,
And mount, by your inspired thoughtes aboue,
* To heauen-ward, home-ward, whence you had your birth:
  Take to you this, that Monarches may envie,
  Your heartes content, and high fœlicitie.

You, you, that over-looke the cloudes of care,
And smile to see a multitude of Antes,
Vppon this circle, striuing here and there,
For THINE and MINE, yet pine amid their wantes;
  While yee your selues, sit as spectators free,
  From action, in their follies tragædie.

* Virtus recludens immeritis mori Cœlum, negata tentat iter via Cœtusque vulgares, et vdam spernit humum fugiente penna: Horac: 3 carm: ode.2.

F2.

191
HENRICVS VIII. ANGLIÆ,
FRANCIÆ ET HYBERNIÆ REX.

CAtaracta sex trabibus constans cum coronâ arcrià catenulis inclusâ, & tali epigraphe : SECVRITAS ALTERA. Figuratur symbolo hoc, non ab vno, sed pluribus subsidijs Regem pendere : idquod omnibus salutariter impera-

193
IDEM.

ROsa, cui imminet corona cum inscriptione: RVTILANS ROSA SINE SPINA Præfert hoc symbolo Rex, omnibus exclusis, vel æmulis, vel gentilibus, se solum rerum potiri, clauumque regni vtiliter citra odium moderari.

L   Rosa

Plates 19 & 20

195
IACOBVS ANGLIÆ, GALLIÆ
SCOTIÆ, ET HYBERNIÆ REX

G Ladius, supra quem corona, cum inscriptione: PRO ME SIME-
RIOR IN ME. *Ex historijs nostrum. Tre-*
iatum Principem sapientem præsectæ præsens
gladium districtu tradidisse ferrāt, additis his
L 2   Hoc

197
IDEM.

C Arduus superaddita epigraphe:
NEMO ME IMPVNE LACESSET.
Innuit, neminem se lacessiturum, neminem
quoq; lacessentem impune laturum. Sicutie-
nim carduus, nisi declines, pungit &
lædit: sic princeps iniustè lacessitus iu-
L 3   stere-

Plates 21 & 22

199
IACOBVS I. STVARTVS REX
SCOTIÆ.

Corona humi posita, supra quam gladi⁹ & crux adnexa gnoma PRO LIGE ET PRO GREGE, Innuitur, Regis esse officiū religionis sinceritatē conseruare, ac subditos à violētiis atq; iniuriis omnis à domesticis

L 4

201
ROBERTVS STVARTVS
REX SCOTIÆ.

SPhæra mundi supra posita corona, & supra eam stella tali cum symbolo: VANITAS VANITATVM ET OMNIA VANITAS. Agnouit hic Rex, quod ægro scire omnes debemus, vitā humanæ etiam felicis

L 5

Plates 23 & 24

207
FRIDERICVS DANIÆ NOR-
VEGIÆ SELAND. GOTHOR. REX.

FOrtuna in pila volubili ſtans & velũ vibrans cum inſcriptione: FEDELTA E COSA RARA. Innuitur hoc clemmate hominum leuitas; qui quemadmodum vento circumagitatur velum: ſic illi animum, quo

209
CHRISTIERNVS SECVNDVS
DANIÆ NORVEGIÆ, SELANdiæ, Gotth. Rex.

AQuila draconem vnguibus tenens cum inſcriptione: DIMICANDVM: Notat Rex aliquem hoſtium, quo cum bellum ſit fortiter gerendum. Verè enim Tullius:
M Duo

LE SENTENTIO-SE IMPRESE, ET DIALO-GO DEL SYMEONE.

Con la verificatione del sito di Gergobia, la Geografia d'Ouernia, la figura & tempio d'Apolline in Velay: & il suo hieroglyfico monumento, natiuità, vita & Epitaffio.

AL SERENISS. DVCA DI SAVOIA.

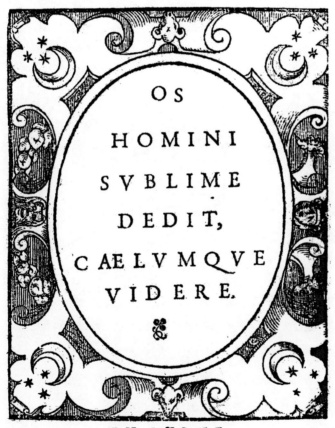

OS
HOMINI
SVBLIME
DEDIT,
CAELVMQVE
VIDERE.

IN LYONE,
APRESSO GVLIELMO ROVIGLIO.
1560.
Con Priuilegio del Rè.

LE
IMPRESE DI M.
GABRIEL SYMEONI
FIORENTINO.
PER I SERENISSIMI DVCA, ET
DVCHESSA DI SAVOIA.

L'vn di Dio porta amore & nome in fronte,
L'altra di ricca Gemma Orientale.
Dotti ambo son, di sangue ogn'vn Reale.
Chi dunque fia che le lor lodi conte?

MORALI.

DEL RE ET REINA
DI NAVARRA.

Il dur Diamante, e i due piu chiari lumi,
   Altro non dicon con vnita fede,
   Se non ch'ei son l'vn, come l'altra herede
Di splendenti, reali, alti costumi.

Simul &
semper.

IMPRESE DEL VESCOVO GIOVIO, RIDOTTE A' MORALITA' DAL MEDESIMO SYMEONE.

DI CARLO V. IMPERATORE.

Ben conuenne à costui l'ardita impresa,
S'Affrica già cognobbe il suo valore,
Ch'anchor nel Regio figlio hoggi non muore,
Mostrando l'alma à maggior fatti accesa.

Plus vlt

f 3

56　　　TETRASTICHI

DI PAPA LIONE X.

Soaue è il giogo, e'l popolo fedele,
　Se il Signor non lo stratia, & non s'adira:
　Ma doue hoggi dal Ciel tal gratia spira,
Et doue nasce senza assentio il mele?

MORALI.

DELL'ALCIATO.

Mai non auenne che l' huòm buono & dotto,
Se ben pare hoggi che l'ignaro sia
Solo essaltato, hauesse carestia,
Ne ch'al vitio virtu stesse di sotto.

DE L'IMPERADOR FERDINANDO · I

Con la scorta di quel ualor profondo,
  Che d'ogni meta e d'ogni segno è fuore;
FERDINANDO, al fratel sù le minore,
  Sperò girare domar tutto il mondo.
Fu di bontate a null'altro secondo,
  E sempre arse nel cor d'santo ardore
  Di render a GESV deuuto honore,
  E d'Europa scacciar il Turco immondo

Morte ui s'interpose, onde no'l feo.
  Ma basta il buon uoler, che lo fa eguale
Aciascun glorioso semideo.
Erado goderà Principe tale
  La consolata Italia, e'l mondo reo,
  Vago me ben lo sà, del proprio male

DEL CAPITAN GIROLAMO MATTHEI ROMANO.

Ha lo Struzzo tal don da la Natura,
Che 'l duro ferro digerisce e pasce:
Cosi, quanto si uoglia acerba e dura
Cosa a Spirito franco unqua non noce.

Quel, che s'oppone al suo ualor, nõ cura:
M'a l'imprese maggior corre ueloce.
Onde con fronte poi di Lauro adorna
Sempre con laude e uincitor ritorna.

DELLA REINA DI FRANCIA.

Se ſtella iniqua ha qui forza e ualore
   D'apportar fra mortali influſſi rei;
La prudenza de l'huomo haue di lei,
   E d'ogni rio deſtin poſſa maggiore.
Onde armata di ſenno e di ualore
   La Reina di Francia; ei ſommi Dei
L'ardir accompagnando di coſtei,
   Eſtinto ha l'Vgonotico furore.

Coſi l'inuitto figlio alto poggiando
   Per le uirtù paterne, a poco a poco
Porrà la ſetta, a Dio nimica, in bando.
   Quinci fia ritornato il primo loco
A la Romana Chieſa; in lui auāpādo
   De lo Spirito Diuin l'ardente foco.

Plate 36

DEL S. GIROLAMO RVSCELLI.

La pianta, ch'è uicina a le chiar'onde
D'alcun bel rio, che le sue riue honori,
Cresce, mercè di Stelle alme e seconde,
Di frutti adorna, e d'odorati fiori:
E le bacche diuengono feconde
Di celeste sapor ne i uerdi Allori.
Cosi cresce il Ruscel con fama chiara,
Mercè di sua uirtute unica, o rara.

SPECVLVM HEROICVM

Principis omnium temporum
Poëtarum.

HOMERI,

*Id est argumenta xxiiij. librorum Iliados
in quibus veri Principis Imago Poëticè,
elegantissime exprimitur.*

LES XXIIII. LIVRES D'HOMERE

Reduict en tables demonstratives figurées, par
Crespin de Passe, excellent graveur.

Chacque livre redigé en argument Poëticque.

Par le Sieur I. Hillaire, Sr de la Riviere, rouennois.

Prostant in Officina CR. PASSAEI *calcographi.*

TRAIECTI BATAVORVM,

Et Arnhemiæ apud Ioannem Ianssonium, Bibliopolam.
ANNO MDCXIII.

LIB. III.	LIV. III.
SINGVLARE HABET PRAELIVM	DEVIL OV SINGVLIERE
Alexandri & Menelai.	bataille entre Alexandre & Menelae.

Causa mali tanti es, tua es causa vna, furoris
Tyndari, quæ lætos cogis ad arma viros.
Infelix pretium pugnæ tua forma futura est.
Et victor justus nempe maritus erit.

BONA CAVSA DIIS CVRÆ.

Dispositi in turmas equitum cuneosq́, pedestres
Argiui Phrygij́q, viri, fera bella minantur:
Cum Priamus reges Helena monstrante, Pelasgos
Cognoscit, laudatq́, duces splendentibus armis
Indutos, Martem totum spirantiaq́, ora.
Committit vates isto mox fædere amantes,
Et statuit justo damnosa præmia formæ
Victori, victum, rapit Phryga nubibus atris
Ipsa Venus, thalamoq́, suo tegit, immemor illa
Fœderis, attonito suadens periuria amanti
Accumulare fuga, pulchram nec linquere prædam.

L'Ost ainsi rasseuré chacun deux se prépare
Le Grec & le Troien en mesme temps armez
Vont au devant de ce qui les rend hallarmez
Vn mur tant seulement l'un & l'autre separe.
Qui a veu quelque fois vn Cavallier Tartare
Panades voltiger a bras nud desarmé
Il a veu Menelaus qui d'Helenne charmé
Bastist vn fort d'amour que la haulte rémpare
Il combat main a main auec le beau berger
Vaincu il faict Paris dessoubz les loix ranger
Alexandre promet de luy rendre sa dame
Heleane courroucée en pesche cest effaict,
Et ce que l'un promist par l'autre fust desfaict
Ne restant au vaincœur q'vne plaie en son ame.

B 3

LIB. VI.	LIV. VI.
HABET HELENI CONSILIVM, ET Hectoris cum Andromache colloquium.	CONTIENT LE CONSEIL DV PROPHEte Helene, ensemble le colloque de Hector & sa femme Andromache.

Dum Græci premerent victores agmina Teucrum,   Priamides suadet surde dare vota Minervæ,
Et gladio caderent millia multa virûm :   6   Et frustra offensam sollicitare Deam.

IN ADVERSIS AD DEORVM recurrendum auxilium.

Quid nunc Sidoneo tentatam Pallada peplo,
Dardanidasq́; nurus venerantes supplice voce
Iratam divam, referam, & pia dona ferentes
Nequicquam ; nec enim quis dura revellere fata
Mortalis poterat, vel Divum sanguine cretus.
Quid ve feram lachrimas Thebeæ coniugis, & te
Parve puer cristas & cassidis æra timentem ?
Aut Glauci insignem Diomedem munere & armis,
Quassantemq́; procul metuendam cuspidis vmbram !
Vel Paridem pulchris comitatû hinc Hectora in armis ?
Quæ tibi dat sexto divinus codice Homerus.

Hecuba & Priam advertis d'Hellenus
Qu'il se falloit armer la bouche de priere
Pour chasser de leurs maux vne partie arriere
A ceste fin aussy le peuple y soict admis
Et les veux promptement seient sur l'autter mis
Hecuba l'œuil baigné au chappellet espere
Et laiant desplie faict ainsy sa prierre
Deesse en qui les dieux tant de pouvoir ont mis
Appaise ton courroux & de nostre infortune
Monstre toy desormaitz benigne & opportune
Tandis Hector fasché releve le debat
Renouvelle le choc Glaucus & Diomede
Combattent entre tant le Ciel forge vn remède
Et les rend bons amis au millieu du combat.

C 2

LIB. XXIIII.	LIV. XXIIII.
A IOVE MONITVS ACHILLES PAtri reddit cadaver Hectoris.	ACHILLE PAR L'ADVERTISSEMENT de Iupiter, rend le corps mort de Hector a Priam.

Dat Thetidi pia iusta patr. Saturnius, iram.
Mitiget ut nati, tumido nec turgidus ore 24
Spernat supplicijs repetentis hunc Hectora verbis:
Sed memor immensum discat moderare furorem.

CESSAT POST FV-
-nera livor.

Vppiter iratus savam Pelidis ob iram,
Et facinus dirum iam detestatur Achillis:
Quod sit grande nefas savire in funera quenquam
Post fatum & deceat indicta ponere metam
Tunc Thetidem nato monitricem mittit Achilli,
Vt memor humana sortis, cohibere furorem
Tentet, & immensum discat compescere fastum.
Cætera prosequitur vates Priamumque superbos
Porrectum ante pedes, atque auro supplice victum
Invictum narrans iuvenem; lamentaq; sava
Iliadum; mæstosq; rogos; cineremq; sepultum.

Ivppiter a Achil' Tetidem il envoie
Affin quil dellaissast de plus tiranniser,
Le corps du preux Hector sans le martiriser,
Ce dieu tout de rechef iris encor renvoie
A Priam, qui Mercur' a remis sur la voie
Qui ces yeux tout baignez ne pouvoit espuiser
De voir ainsy d'Hector, la gloire mespriser
Qui feust iadis l'honneur de la superbe Troie,
Achill' eust sa ransonqui monta autant d'or
Que pesoit le corps mort puis qu'un drap de fin or,
Ce grand Martz feust couvert & mis en sepulture
Par miracle divin les mortz l'aunis palmiers
Q'on planta sur sa tombe avecq les lauriers,
Repprindent a l'instant leur premiere nature.

Fin des 24. LIV. d'Homere.

INTRODUCTION.

A BRIEF REVIEW OF ENGLISH EMBLEM-BOOKS PREVIOUS TO A.D. 1618, AND OF THE MIRROR OF MAJESTY ITSELF.

I.

EMBLEM-BOOKS by English authors have never been numerous, and seldom original in their conception and execution. The ground was occupied by the writers of Italy, France, and Germany, and thence were works of an emblematic character transplanted to England, receiving such pruning and dressing as might accommodate them to another climate and soil. Our elder poets indeed make it evident that there was no deficiency among us of fancy to devise and of language to express thoughts in emblems. Chaucer's Prioress (*Cant. Tales*, v. 160) had

> "a broche of gold full shene,
> On which was first ywriten a crouned A,
> And after, *Amor vincit omnia*."

The *Romaunt of the Rose* abounds in allegorical descriptions, among which may especially be named, THE GOD OF LOVE, and his "bachelere" SWETE LOOKING, with "turke bowes two," and "ten brode arrowes" in two bundles. In five of them, v. 948;

> "all was golde men might see,
> Out-take the feathers and the tree."

> "The swiftest of these arrowes five
> Out of a bow for to drive,
> And beste feathered for to flie,
> And fairest eke, was cleped Beautie."

The *Well of Love* is afterwards described, *v.* 1567, and the writer says,—

> "Downe at the bottome set saw I
> Two cristal stones craftely
> In thilke fresh and faire well,
> But o thing soothly dare I tell."

The "two cristal stones" are the one "the mirrour perillus"; the other the mirrour in which among a thousand things more he saw, *v.* 1651,—

> "A roser charged full of roses
> That with an hedge about encloses."

The monk of Bury St. Edmunds, John Lydgate, afterwards to be mentioned, in his rendering of the *Dance of Macaber* into English rhymes, presents no less than four subjects for emblems in his four lines on *God's Providence*.

> "God hath a thousand handés to chastise,
> A thousand dartés of punicion;
> A thousand bowés made in divers wise;
> A thousand arblasts bent in his dongèon."

The Turns of Fortune, by Sir Thomas Wyatt, need but "the pictures and short poesies" to be rendered into very expressive emblems; as—

> "He is not dead that sometime had a fall!
> The sun returns that hid was under cloud,
> And when fortune hath spit out all her gall,
> I trust good luck to me shall be allowed;
> For I have seen a ship in haven full,
> After the storm had broke both mast and shroud.
> The willow eke, that stoopeth with the wind
> Doth rise again, and greater wood doth bind."

So also might be rendered, from Dunbar's *Dance of the seven deadly Sins,* the expressive lines, where

> "—— first of all in dance was Pride,
> With hair coiled back and bonnet on side,
> Like to make vaistie wanes;

>   And round about him as a wheel,
>   Hung all in rumples to the heel,
>   His kethat for the nanes.
>   Mony proud trompour with him trippit;
>   Through scalding fire ay as they skippit,
>   They girned with hideous granes."

Lastly, Lord Sackville's description of Misery, Sleep, and Old Age, at the beginning of the *Mirrovr for Magistrates*, shows how readily proverb and picture might be employed to give to portions of his work all the characteristics of emblematical device. Misery's plight has been portrayed, and the graphic description thus goes on :—

>   "By him lay heevy Sleep, the cousin of death,
>   Flat on the ground, and still as any stone,
>   A very corpse save yielding forth a breath :
>   Small kepe took he whom Fortune frownéd on;
>   Or whom she lifted up into the throne
>   Of high renown; but as a living death,
>   So dead alive, of life he drew the breath."

If we may rely on the testimony of Neugebaverus in his *Selectorum Symbolorvm Heroicvm Centvria gemina*, Francfort, 1619,* a year only after the *Mirrovr of Maiestie*, there were Emblems in use by ENGLISH SOVEREIGNS as early as the conquest of England by the Duke of Normandy. To William I., king of England, he assigns a Lion erect and preparing to meet an engine of war, and two spears,—the motto FORTITER RESISTENDVM, *Bravely must we withstand.*

Henry I. has a ladder, the motto, PER GRADVS VELOX, *Swift by the steps.*
Henry II. an anchor erect, FATA VIAM INVENIENT, *The fates will find a way.*

---

* A work of very similar character, of which we have the beautiful 12th edition, 1666, before us, had appeared in 1601, 1602, and 1603, containing about 350 Emblems, with their mottoes and devices. The title is "SYMBOLA DIVINA ET HUMANA Pontificvm Imperatorum Regum; et Symbola varia diversorum principum; Ex musæo Octavii de Strada, cum Isagoge Iac. Typotii, &c." *Egidius Sadeler. Pragæ.* Fol. The selection by Neugebaverus is greatly indebted to the *Symbols divine and human* of Octavius de Strada.

There are also about 160 mottoes, devices, and quatrains without pictures, *i. e.* 160 *nude* Emblems, in Le Vassevr's "DEVISES DES EMPEREVRS ROMAINS, tant Italiens que Grecs & Allemans, depuis Iules Cæsar iusques a Rodolphe II. à present regnant." 12mo., pp. 80. "A Paris, M.DCVIII."

Edward I., King of England and Ireland, a covered enclosure, HINC FORTIVS IBO, *Hence more bravely will I go.*
Edward II., a spider's web, with ARDENTIOR IBO, *More eagerly will I go.*
Edward III., King of England, France, and Ireland, a whale sporting with little fishes, ASSENTATIONE MORIOR, *By flattery I die.*
Richard II., a serpent twined about stalks of laurel and palm, that form an oval wreath with a crown above, REGIS VICTORIÆ AC VIRTVTIBUS, *For the king's victory and virtues.*
Henry IV., an altar supporting an erect sword and crown, PRO ARA ET REGNI CVSTODIA, *For the altar and safety of the kingdom.*
Henry V., an eagle holding a garland in its beak, IMPERII SPES ALTA FVTVRI, *The high hope of future empire.*
Henry VII., a crane with one leg on a globe, and in the other grasping a stone, NON DORMIT QVI CVSTODIT, *He sleeps not who guards.*
Henry VIII., a portcullis of six beams, surmounted by a crown, SECVRITAS ALTERA, *A double safeguard;* also, the rose and crown; RVTILANS ROSA SINE SPINA, *The red rose without a thorn.*

From another source (*Gentleman's Magazine*, 1819, pt. ii. pp. 130–131; and 1826, pt. ii. pp. 201–203), we learn that, on some occasions, Henry VII. adopted, for his badge, the white and red roses in union; and on other occasions, in reference to Bosworth field, the crown in a bush: Henry VIII. made use also of the device of an archer drawing his arrow to the head; Edward VI. chose for himself a sun, or the phœnix, with the motto, NASCATVR VT ALTER, *That another may be born.* Mary, as princess, preferred the white and red rose and a pomegranate knotted together; as queen, Time drawing truth out of a well, the words being VERITAS TEMPORIS FILIA, *Truth the daughter of time.* Of Elizabeth's badges we find mentioned her mother's falcon,* or rather dove; and the crown and sceptre, but most frequently a sieve. Among the mottoes were SEMPER EADEM, *Always the same,* and VIDEO ET TACEO, *I see and am silent.*

The foregoing account of Emblems or Badges adopted by the Sovereigns of England, is very far indeed from being exhaustive, neither is it to be regarded as possessing absolute certainty. Many might be added,—some might be controverted,—but for such as have been mentioned, the authority relied on has been adduced.

* In *Symb. div. et hum.*, ed. 1673, p. 302, Queen Anna Boleyn has for device a star shining within the serpent-circle, surmounted by a crown, and on the scroll FATO PRVDENTIA MAIOR, *Wisdom greater than fate.*

BADGES OF ENGLISH NOBLES. 69

The nobles too and gentry of England followed the example of the sovereigns, in appropriating to themselves, each a badge or device, and motto. A manuscript in the British Museum (Bibl. Cotton Claudius, CIII. Plut. xxi. F. 4), *Names and Arms of Knights* from 1485 to 1624, gives many undoubted proofs of heraldic devices; and *the Covntesse of Pembroke's Arcadia; written by Sir Philippe Sidnei*, proves by the mottoes and devices on the shields of the knights, the abundant knowledge of the subject and readiness of invention which the author possessed. Amply sufficient, however, on this point is it to adduce the authority of Sir William Stirling-Maxwell, in his admirable introduction to the *Chief Victories of the Emperor Charles the Fifth*, p. xxiiia, where he speaks of the Emperor's "usual and favourite device," *the Pillars and Plus ultra*, as "one of the most famous of its class":—"when such inventions were held in high esteem," and "the noble gentlemen of Europe, in adorning their glorious triumphs, declared their inward pretensions, purposes, and enterprizes, not by speech or any apparent manner, but shadowed under a certain veil of forms and figures," and "when it was the fashion for men of all degrees to clothe in symbolic shape their sympathies or antipathies, their sorrows, joys, or affections, or the hopes and ambitions of their lives." To set forth then a *Mirrovr of Maiestie*, like the work now reproduced, was simply to collect together the recognized distinctions of rank, or in some cases to invent, as in many previous instances, the devices and the mottoes which were deemed suitable to the persons represented.

In the CENTVRIA GEMINA, *the double hundred of Choice Heroic Symbols*, before quoted from, are several Emblems assigned to kings of Scotland and of Denmark; these we purpose introducing among the plates illustrative of the *Mirrovr of Maiestie;* but we will here simply note down what Peacham testifies in his *Minerva Britanna*, ed. 1612.

"Who hath ever seene," he asks, "more wittie, proper, and significant devises than those of *Scotland?* (to omit more auncient times) as that of *King*

James the third, devising for himselfe (to expresse the care he had of his country and People) a *Hen* sitting over her *Chickens*, with the word *Non dormit qui custodit;* as also *James* the fowrth taking to himself a bifront, or double face, plac't vpon the top of a Columne : the heades crowned with *Laurell*, the word *Vtrumque:* meaning (as it is thought) he would constantly and advisedly, like *Janus*, observe the proceedings as well of the *French* as the *English*, holding them both at that time in Ielousie. Many and very excellent have I seene of his *Maiesties* owne Invention,* who hath taken herein in his younger years great delight and pleasure, by which thou maiest see, that we are not so dull as they would imagine us, nor our Soule so barren as that we neede to borrow from their Sunne-burnt braines our best Invention."

Of early ENGLISH-EMBLEM BOOKS a prominent place may be assigned to 𝕿𝖍𝖊 𝕱𝖎𝖇𝖊 𝖂𝖔𝖚𝖓𝖉𝖘 𝖔𝖋 𝕮𝖍𝖗𝖎𝖘𝖙. 𝕭𝖞 𝖂𝖎𝖑𝖑𝖎𝖆𝖒 𝕭𝖞𝖑𝖑𝖎𝖓𝖌,† written between the years 1400 and 1430. The original, according to William Bateman, of Darby, near Matlock, the editor of the 4to Manchester edition, 1814,—is "a finely illuminated parchment roll of about two yards and three quarters in length." There are seven illuminated and seven outline plates, and the texts bordered at the sides by a pinnacle and statue,—on the top by a cherub between two death's heads,—and at the foot by an unclothed skeleton lying on the ground.

The fourth illuminated picture is of a wounded hand with golden rays issuing from it; on the scroll is emblazoned the line "𝖎𝖍𝖋 𝖙𝖍𝖊 𝖜𝖊𝖑𝖑 𝖔𝖋 𝖌𝖗𝖆𝖈𝖊," and below the stanza :—

---

* From one of the king's letters, dated at Newcastle, on his journey to take possession of his English throne, it is evident that he busied himself with issuing commands for the striking of several new coins against the time of his coronation. He minutely describes the arms, quarterings, and mottoes, and while his name and titles were to be around his head, he chose as the *word* for the shield EXVRGAT DEVS DISSIPENTVR INIMICI, *Let God arise and my enemies shall be scattered.* With such facts we need not cancel the rendering of the word *"devise"* in some lines quoted in *Shakespeare and the Emblem Writers*, p. 122 :—

"*Maintenant, devise, & coquette,*
Régi par la Reine Jaquette."
Now, chitter-chatter and Emblemes
Ruled by our Queen, the little James.

† A writer in *Notes and Queries*, Jan. 30th, 1869, p. 103, on mentioning the monogram 𝖂𝖎𝖑𝖑𝖒 𝕭𝖎𝖑𝖑𝖞𝖓𝖌, says, "I take it, then, that Billyng was only the copier of the poems, not the author." Under the date March 6th, 1869, p. 229, we are informed by Llewellyn Jewett, "that the original parchment is at Lomberdale House."

> "Hayle welle of grace most precyouse in honoure
> In the kynges left hande set of ierusalem
> Swettur thanne bawme is thy swete lycore
> Whiche in largesse to us doth owt estreme
> So precius a flode is in no kynges reame
> Of perfyte grace thow art restoratyfe
> And in alle vtu most preseruatyfe."

At the end of the work are *six* stanzas beginning,

> "Erth owte of erth is worderly wroght
> Ffor orth hath geten of erth a nohul thyng of noght
> Erth uppon erthe hath set alle hys thoght
> How erthe uppon erthe may be hygh broght."

About the same time with Billyng flourished John Lydgate, Monk of Bury, who, it is said, wrote above 250 poems,* the greater part, however, of only a few leaves in extent. He died in 1460 and is now chiefly remembered for introducing into English rhymes *The Daunce of Machabre*, London, 1554, and given by Douce in the reprint of 1790. "Whereon is lively expressed and shewed The state of manne, And how he is called at uncertayne tymes by Death, and when he thinketh least thereon."

Under Henry VI. Lydgate's verses were set up in the great cloister on the north side of the old cathedral church of St. Paul, London, to explain the personages who took part in the Dance or March of Death, which had been painted there on the walls. They were preserved in this place until the reign of Edward VI., when, according to Stowe's *Survey of London*, edition 1720, vol. i. bk. 3, p. 145, "in the year 1549, on the 10th of April, the said Chappel, by Commandement of the Duke of *Somerset*, was begun to be pulled down, with the whole Cloister, the Dance of Death, the Tombs and Monuments."

Another work "by Ihn Lidgate Monke of Berry" was printed at London in 1614; a folio of 318 pages in double columns; it is "THE LIFE AND DEATH OF HECTOR; One and the first of *the most Puissant*,

---

* In Speght's *Workes of our antient and learned English Poet Geffrey Chaucer*, London, 1598, at folio 398 there is an account, or rather catalogue, of Lydgate's *Translations and Poetical Devises*.

Valiant, and Renowned Monarches *of the world called the Nyne worthies.*" Within the richly ornamented title-page the anachronism is committed of placing the escutcheon of America on a book first dedicated "vnto the high *and mightie Prince* HENRY the Fift."

Some evidence of Lydgate's knowledge of device may be adduced from Dugdale's *Monasticon Anglicanum*, edition 1849, iii., Note 99, p. 104. Besides the numerous limnings, one hundred and twenty, on his MS. Life of St. Edmund, "which formerly belonged to King Henry VI., are representations of TWO BANNERS, feigned by the poet to have been borne by St. Edmund in his war against the Danes. The first represents Adam and Eve by the tree of life, about to eat the forbidden fruit, which is reached to the woman by the serpent, who appears down the middle with a human shape. Above is the Holy Lamb with a gold circle and a glory about its head; its right foot bearing up a golden cross fleurée fitchée. The red ground of this banner within the circle which contains the Lamb is powdered with crescents, and without with stars, all of gold, as is the tree itself. The figures of the woman, serpent, and man, the apples and the Lamb, are all of silver. The second banner represents the coat of arms belonging to the abbey, *Az.* three crowns *Or:* the crowns, according to the poet, signifying royal dignity, virginity, and martyrdom. Lydgate represents St. Edmund to have used this banner 'at Geynesburuhe.'"

Sir Thomas More, who was born in 1480, has left sufficient proof of his knowledge of Emblem-writings and of his power to imitate them. What he did in this way are indeed only fragments executed by him about A.D. 1495 or 1496, and the pictorial delineations themselves have perished with the fair cloth on which they were painted. From his Works,* printed in 1557, we extract the following notice :—

* Within a monumental border the title runs : "THE vvorkes of Sir *Thomas More Knight, some tyme Lorde Chancellour of England, wrytten by him in the Englysh tonge.* Printed at *London at the costes and charges of Iohn Cawood, Iohn Waly, and Richarde Tottel.* Anno 1557." Small folio. Initial pages 36, unnumbered, 1—1458 numbered; total pp. 1494.

"Mayster Thomas More in his youth devysed in hys fathers house in London, a goodly hangyng of fyne paynted clothe, with nyne pageauntes, and verses ouer of euery of these pageauntes: which verses expressed and declared, what the ymages in those pageauntes represented: and also in those pageauntes were paynted, the thynges that the verses ouer them dyd (in effecte) declare, which verses here followe."

The subjects of these "nyne pageauntes," all written in English, except the last, which is in Latin, are Chyldhod, Manhod, Venus and Cuppyde, Age, Deth, Fame, Tyme, Eternitee, and The Poet.*

"In the sixt pageant was painted lady Fame. And vnder her fete was the picture of Death that was in the fifth pageant. And ouer this sixt pageaunt the writyng was as foloweth:—

"¶ FAME.

Fame I am called, maruayle you nothing,
Though with tonges am compassed all rounde
For in voyce of people is my chiefe liuyng.
O cruel death, thy power I confounde.
When thou a noble man hast brought to grounde
Maugry thy teeth to lyue cause hym shall I,
Of people in perpetuall memory."

The progress which books of Emblems made in England may next be marked by two translations from Brandt's Narren Schyff, Bâle, 1494, which were printed in London in the year 1509. The *one* rendered through the French by Henry Watson, THE SHYPPE OF FOOLES, came from the press of "Wynkyn de Worde MCCCCCIX"; the *other*, through Latin, French, and German, by Alexander Barclay, The Shyp of Folys of the Worlde was "Imprinted in the Cyte of London by Richard Pynson M.D.IX." Barclay's translation was repeated in 1570 by Cawood, "Printer to the Queenes Maiestie." Of the style of this work we may judge by the Foolish Book-Collector's description of his own pursuits.

* *See* Dibdin's *Typ. Antiquities*, ii. p. 431.

"I am the first foole of all the whole Navie
To keepe the Pompe, the Helme, and eke the Sayle :
For this is my minde, this one pleasure have I,
Of bookes to have great plentie and apparayle.
I take no wisdome by them, nor yet avayle,
Nor them perceave not, and then I them despise ;
Thus am I a foole, and all that sue that guise.

That on this Ship the chief place I governe
By this wide Sea with fooles wandring,
The cause is plaine and easy to discerne,
Still am I busy bookes assembling,
For to have plentie, it is a pleasaunt thing
In my conceyt, and to have them ay in hande ;
But what they meane do I not understande."

Barclay was priest, or chaplain of the college of Ottery St. Mary, Devonshire, and afterwards monk of Ely. Hazlitt's *Hand-Book*, p. 25, supplies evidence that he "was employed by Henry VIII. to compose the impressas, &c. used at the Field of Cloth of Gold," A.D. 1520. To the 1570 edition of *the Shyp of Folys of the Worlde* is attached an Emblematical work translated from Dominicus Mancinus, *Libellus de quattuor virtutibus*, edition 1484 : it is entitled, " *The Mirrour of Good Maners*," "containing the foure Cardinal Vertues." *The Myrrour of good Maners*, however, was first printed by " Rychard Pynson," and then with the types of Wynkyn de Worde, *circa* 1516.

The year 1520 gave welcome to an English version of the 𝔇𝔶𝔞𝔩𝔬𝔤𝔲𝔰 𝔒𝔯𝔢𝔞𝔱𝔲𝔯𝔞𝔯𝔲𝔪,—a collection of Latin fables, to which, in the fourteenth century, was appended the name of Nicolas Pergaminus, and which was first printed by Gerard Leeu, at Gouda, in 1480. The English title is *The Dialoges of Creatures moralyzed*, " of late trãslated out of latyn in to our Englysshe tonge, right profitable to the gouernaunce of man." Of the 122 devices in simple outline the *Shakespeare Emblems*, p. 52, offer two examples : *The Sun and the Moon*, and *The Wolf and the Ass*. In the Royal Library at the Hague there is a beautifully-illuminated copy of the original work. Haslewood in 1816 reprinted 100 copies ; but above half were destroyed by an accidental fire, and thus the reprint itself, though very modern, is very rare.

Assuming, as we may do, that devices followed by stanzas are characteristics of Emblem-Books, there may here be named in the series, *Quadins historiques de la Bible*, Historic Picture-frames of the Bible, with designs by "the little Bernard," published at Lyons between 1553 and 1583. Of these there was an English version; and at Lyons, in 1553, appeared " *The true and lyuely Portreatures of the woll Bible* (translated into English metre by Peter Dorendel)."

A short time before, in 1549, had also been issued by John Frellon, of Lyons, " *The Images of the Old Testament,* —set forthe in Ynglishe and French, vuith a playn and brief exposition"; and this work may be said to have had its herald in 1535, when *Storys and Prophesis* were "prentyd in Andwarpe."

The pretty little volume by William de la Perrière, *Le Theatre des bons Engins*, auquel sont contenu cent Emblemes," bears the date, Paris 1539; but except "a fragment of an English translation" in the noble Emblem Library at Keir, in Scotland, no English version is known; but by the cast of the type and by the woodcuts, this English translation "*might* be of the sixteenth century, and probably as early as Daniell's *Jovius*."

According to Ames's *Antiquities of Printing*, Herbert's edition, p. 1570, the Emblems of the famous Italian lawyer, Andrew Alciat, were published in an English version in 1551 ; but this account is very apocryphal, and as yet unsupported by other testimony.

GLI TRIUMPHI DEL PETRARCHA, Triumphs of Love, Chastity, and Death, had, in the Venice editions of 1500 and 1523, been adorned with vignettes and wood-engravings; but it was not until about the year 1560 that the work was translated into English, also with wood-engravings, and bore the title " *The Tryumphes of Fraunces Petrarcke*," "by Henry Parker knyg[ht], lorde Morley."*
The long popularity of Petrarch's *Triumphi* is attested by

---

* "On 25th Nov., 1556, he, by the death of his aged grandfather succeeded to the barony of Morley." "He died 22 Oct., 1577." For particulars of him see *Athenæ Cantabrigienses*, i. pp. 378 and 566.

English translations in 1644, 1807, 1836, and 1859, to which are attached the names of Mrs. Anne Hume, Henry Boyd, Lady Dacre, and Thomas Campbell.

The allegorical, not to name them the emblematical *Visions of Petrarch*, as well as those of Bellay, Spenser exhibited at an early period of his life. These, together with *the Visions of the World's Vanitie*, present "a series of Emblems."* We subjoin one of them, *The Phœnix*, from Petrarch :—

> "I saw a Phœnix in the wood alone,
>   With purple wings, and crest of golden hewe;
>   Strange bird he was, whereby I thought anone,
>   That of some heavenly wight I had the vewe;
>   Untill he came unto the broken tree,
>   And to the spring, that late devoured was.
>   Why say I more? each thing at last we see
>   Doth passe away : the Phœnix there alas,
>   Spying the tree destroid, the water dride,
>   Himselfe smote with his beake, as in disdaine,
>   And so foorthwith in great despight he dide;
>   That yet my heart burnes, in exceeding paine,
>   For ruth and pitie of so haples plight :
>   O ! let mine eyes no more see such a sight."

Emblems, as the author names them, or posies, are added to each part of *The Shepheards Calender*, and the structure of the eclogues or tales bears directly upon the subjects. Take Colin's *Emblem for November*, LA MORT NY MORD, *death byteth not*, and follow up the tale of Dido's death until

> "She hath the bonds broke of eternall night."

And—

> "—— raignes a goddesse now emong the saintes
>   That whilome was the saynt of shepheards light,
>   And is enstalled nowe in heavens hight.
>   I see thee, blessed soule ! I see
>   Walk in Elisian fieldes so free.
>   O happy herse !
>   Might I once come to thee, (O that I might !)
>   O ioyfull verse."

---

* See Spenser's *Life* prefixed to Moxon's 1856 edition of his works, pp. x. and xi.

It is to be noted how every part of the narrative conduces to the exposition of the theme, *death byteth not.*

"For," adds the author, "although by course of nature we be borne to die, and being ripened with age, as with timely harvest, we must be gathered in time; . . . yet death is not to be coveted for evill, nor (as the Poet said a litle before) as doome of ill desert. For though the trespasse of the first man brought death into the world, as the guerdon of sinne, yet being overcome by the death of one that died for all, it is now made (as Chaucer saith) the greene pathway of life. So that it agreeth well with that was saide, that Death byteth not (that is) hurteth not at all."

Among the early treatises on Emblems the first place is to be assigned to Paolo Giovio's DIALOGO *dell Imprese Militari et Amore;* or, as it is sometimes entitled, RAGIONAMENTO, *Discourse concerning the words and devices of arms and of love, which are commonly named Emblems.* Closely allied in subject and in treatment are Ruscelli's DISCORSO, Venice, 1556, and Domenichi's RAGIONAMENTO, of the same city and year.

The correspondence of Sir Philip Sidney with Languet in 1572 shows that he was acquainted with Ruscelli's *Imprese illustri;* and the mottoes and devices in the *Arcadio,* as we have noticed, give evidence of his general knowledge of the Emblem Art. The knowledge spread in his native land, and in 1585 to the English reader was offered "THE WORTHY TRACT OF PAULUS IOUIUS, contayning a Discourse of rare inuentions both Militarie and Amorous *called Imprese. Whereunto is added a Preface,* contayning the Arte of composing them, with *many other notable deuises. By Samuell Daniell late Student* in Oxenforde."

As a specimen of Giovio's *Worthy Tract* we select a passage in Daniell's translation, where Lorenzo the Magnificent is spoken of as symbolizing Faith, Hope, and Charity. Giovio himself is the speaker, and says:—

"I cănot go beyond the three Diamăts which the great *Cosimo* did leave, which you see engraven in the chamber wherein I lye. But to tell you the trueth, although with all diligêce I have searched, yet cănot I find precisely what they signifie ; & thereof also doubted Pope Clemĕt, who in his meaner fortune lay also in the self same chamber. And trueth it is that he sayd, the *Magnifico Lorenzo* vsed one of them with greate brauerie, inserting it betweene three feathers of three sundrie colours, greene, white and red : which betokened three vertues, Faith, Hope and Charitie, appropriate to those three colours : Hope, greene ; Faith, white; Charitie, red ; with the worde *Semper* belowe it. Which *Impresa* hath bene used of all the successors of his house, yea, and of the Pope : who did beare it imbrodered on the vpper garments of the horsmen of his garde, vnder that of the yoke."

Of Doni's three Emblem works, I MONDI, *the Worlds ;* I MARMI, *the Marbles ;* and LA MORAL FILOSOFIA, *Moral Philosophy*, all printed at Venice, 1552-53, the last, "𝕿𝖍𝖊 𝕸𝖔𝖗𝖆𝖑𝖑 𝕻𝖍𝖎𝖑𝖔𝖘𝖔𝖕𝖍𝖎𝖊 𝖔𝖋 𝕯𝖔𝖓𝖎, drawne out of the auncient writers," "was englished out of italien by Sir Th. North." It is a 4to, printed in 1570 and again in 1601, and was dedicated to Robert, Earl of Leicester, the patron of Whitney's Emblems.

In the Colophon, North's translation declares, " Here endeth the Treatise of the Morall Philosophie of Sendebar." Now the Parables of Sendebar, or Sendebad, were a Hebrew work, says Brunet, v. 294, which was itself derived from the Arabic version of a work originally composed in India, and identical with the Fables of Bidpay, or Pilpay. Among translations of Bidpay are ranked Doni's *Moral Filosofia*, and North's English version. (See Brunet's *Manuel*, i. 936, 938, 939.)

Another most popular book of Emblems, and most deservedly so, was the little volume by Claude Paradin, canon of Beaujeu,—DEVISES HEROIQUES, Lyons, 1557. With motto, woodcut, and prose description, it furnishes much information, and abounds in interesting details. To whom the initials P. S. belong, that appear as those of the English translator, London, 1591, is not ascertained ; nor do Lowndes, J. Payne Collier, and W. Carew Hazlitt, venture on a conjecture. The title is, " *The Heroicall Devises of M. Clavdivs Paradin, Canon of Beauieu,* Whereunto are added the Lord Gabriel Symeons and others." It is very generally acknowledged that Shakespeare was acquainted with this translation, and probably with the original.

The paths of the Herald and of the Emblematist, even if they do not run into one another and cross and double, are so close together as not to be distinguishable in all instances. We may, therefore, here give place to a notice of a black-letter book of no mean fame, which first appeared with woodcuts and other illustrations, on the last day of December, 1562;—namely, " Gerard Leigh's 𝔄𝔠𝔠𝔢𝔡𝔢𝔫𝔰 𝔬𝔣 𝔄𝔯𝔪𝔬𝔯𝔭, Imprinted at London in Fletestrete within Temple barre, at the signe of the hande and starre, by Richard Tottill." After two editions in 1591 and 1597, the work was re-issued with numerous heraldic woodcuts and ornaments, THE ACCIDENCE OF ARMORIE, sm. 4to, 1612.

Vander Noot's *Theatre auquel sont exposés et montrés les inconveniens et miseres qui suiuent les mondains et vicieux, &c.*, bears the imprint "Londres chez Iean Day 1568," and is dedicated to Queen Elizabeth. This work was followed the next year, 1569, by an English version, attributed to Henry Bynneman. (See Hazlitt's *Hand-Book*, p. 625, for the full title.) It is very noteworthy, that at the beginning of the volume there are twenty-one epigrams and sonnets, illustrated by woodcuts, which Spenser translated at an early period of his life; for "he was matriculated" (see *Ath. Cantabrigienses*, ii. p. 258) "as a sizar of Pembroke Hall, 20 May, 1569," when, according to the received biography, he was only sixteen years of age. The translations, to which we have before alluded, p. 76, were from Petrarch and Joachim du Bellay; and by reference to *Les Oeuvres du Bellay*, ed. à Rouen, 1592, Spenser's renderings, although the earliest of his labours, are found to be both exact and spirited.

Of closer agreement than any preceding work in English, with an Emblem-book's form and subjects, was Geffrey Whitney's " CHOICE OF EMBLEMES AND OTHER DEVICES, For the moste part gathered out of sundrie writers, Englished and Moralized, And divers newly devised." "Imprinted at Leyden M.D.LXXXVI." 4to. Whitney was a native of Cheshire, and his work bears evidence to his learning. To each of his 248 Emblems, except one at p. 61, there is a woodcut as well as a motto, and one or more stanzas. The work is confessedly a compilation, and above 220 of the mottoes and devices have been traced to their original sources; indeed 202 are identical with those of the five emblematists, Andrew Alciat, 1492–1550; Claude Paradin, 1510–1590; John Sambucus, 1531–1583; Hadrian Junius, 1511–1575; and Gabriel Faerno, who died in 1561 in the prime of life;* and twenty-three others are gathered out of sundry other writers.

A rank among Emblem-works is claimed by Abraham Fraunce, author of the *Lamentations of Amyntas*, 1587, for his 4to volume printed in London in 1588, and entitled INSIGNIVM, ARMORVM, EMBLEMATVM, HIEROGLYPHICORVM, ET SYMBOLORUM, quæ ab Italis *Imprese* nominantur, explicatio." The Explication is in three books: I. Concerning Insignia; II. Concerning Arms; III. Concerning Symbols, Emblems, and Hieroglyphics. "It does not appear," remarks Joseph Brooks Yates, of Liverpool (see *Lit. and Phil. Society*, 1849), "that he composed any Emblems in English": and "this work consists very much of Heraldic deductions and of conventional rules and distinctions which had been discussed very largely by former writers. Moreover it ought to be classed rather with the treatises on Devices and Symbols than among Books of Emblems."

A similar judgment, and if we follow J. Payne Collier's *Bibliographical and Critical Catalogue of early English Literature*, vol. ii. p. 549, a far more severe judgment, must be pronounced on Wyrley's TRUE VSE OF ARMORIE shewed by Historie and plainly proued by example, &c." pp. 169, London, 4to, 1592. The work contains woodcuts of "Banners, Ensignes, and markes of noblenes and chevalrie"; but according to Collier's just criticism, "it really possesses no merit but of a technical kind, and the two long poems, of which it mainly consists, are about the worst performances in verse that appeared at a date remarkable for the excellence of its poetry."

---

* For full information respecting Geffrey Whitney himself, his family, and his Emblems, with their origin, reference is made to the *fac-simile* REPRINT of 1866, 4to, pp. lxxxviij and 440; *with an Introductory Dissertation, Essays Literary and Bibliographical, and Explanatory Notes*, by Henry Green, M.A.

In his *Wits Commonwealth*, Meres accounts Combe, Whitney, and Willet, as worthy to be compared with "these Emblematists, Andreas Alciatus, Reusnerus, and Sambucus." The Emblem-works of Thomas Combe are generally supposed to have perished, but W. Carew Hazlitt's *Hand-Book*, p. 116, preserves the title thus :— "The theater of fine Devices, cōteyning 100 morall emblems, translated out of Fr. by Tho. Combe. Licensed to Rich. Field in 1592." Not a word of comment is added; but the title itself, and the phrase "translated out of Fr.," induce the inquiry, Was the French work from which Combe made his version La Perrière's *Theatre des bons Engins auquel sont contenus cent Emblemes?* And if so, is not the fragment of an English translation of La Perrière, which Sir William Stirling-Maxwell possesses, a relic of Combe's work? The conjecture receives countenance of truth from Hazlitt's notice of Guillaume de PERRIER, p. 453;—"1. Emblems. Translated into English. *Circa* 1591. 16mo. No perfect copy has been found. (Combe.)"

Andrew Willet, named as we have mentioned in *Wits Commonwealth*, is greatly praised in Fuller's *Worthies*, i. 238. Hazlitt, *Hand-Book*, p. 657, confounds Andrew with Rowland Willet, of Hart Hall, Oxford; but though the author's name does not appear on the title-page of the Emblems, the dedication to Robert Devereux, Earl of Essex, who was elected chancellor of Cambridge 10th of August, 1598,* and the printing of SACRORVM EMBLEMATVM CENTVRIA VNA, by John Legate, printer to the university of Cambridge, even were there not also positive testimony, show the work to have been the production of Andrew, and not of Rowland Willet. The volume itself is a quarto of 84 pages, but the Emblems are *nude*, that is, without woodcuts.

To each Emblem there are usually appended a motto, a text from Scripture, some Latin verses, and then a translation into English. The Dedication to the Earl of Essex occupies four pages, and the *first Emblem* is curiously

* See *Athenæ Cantabrigienses*, ii. p. 298.

laudatory of Queen Elizabeth: "Boni principis encomium," *the praise of a good Prince*. Like the fanciful stanzas of Simias the Rhodian, this Emblem has its Latin verses of 24 lines, arranged in the form of a clipped stunted tree, as given in the reprint of *Whitney's Emblemes*, p. xx., where, by going down the left hand of the lines and taking the first letter of each line, and then up the right hand of the lines and taking the last letter of each line, the acrostic is formed: ELISABETHAM REGINAM DIV NOBIS SERVET IESVS INCOLVMEM. AMEN.—*Elisabeth queen long for us may Jesus keep unharmed. Amen.*

The title is a long one, yet, because of the rarity of the work, we subjoin it:—

"SACRORVM EMBLEMATVM CENTVRIA VNA, quæ tam ad exemplum aptè expressa sunt, et ad aspectum pulchrè depingi possunt, quam quæ aut à veteribus accepta, aut inventa ab aliis hactenus extant. In tres classes distributa, quarum prima emblemata Typica, sive Allegorica: Altera historica, sivè re gesta: Tertia Physica à rerum natura sumpta continet. Omnia à purissimis Scripturæ fontibus derivata, et Anglo-latinis versibus reddita. Ezechielis cap. iiij. vers. j.—ij.

"Ex officina Johannis Legate florentissimæ Academiæ Cantabrigiensis Typographi." 4to. *circa* 1598.

The 67th Emblem, "Puerorum educatio," *the education of boys*, affords a specimen of Willet's English style:—

> " A Scholler must in youth be taught,
> And three things keepe in minde ful sure,
> God's worship that it first be sought,
> And manners then with knowledge pure;
> In Church, in scoole, at table must he
> Deuout, attent, and handsome be."

Of Andrew Willet, Collier's *Early English Literature*, vol. ii. p. 524, gives an estimate and examples, but omits perhaps the most beautiful of his emblems, the 37th,—*Christ instantly present to him who prays aright*. The lines are as follow:—

> "The curtains wrought with pictures were
> hanging in holy place;
> The Cherubs did with wings appeare,
> and gave a goodly grace.
> The house of prayer Angels frequent,
> and Christ him selfe is there,
> Then seeing these are alwayes present
> we ought to pray with feare."

THE MIRROVR OF POLICIE. 83

Certainly of Emblem proclivities is the curious work which is next mentioned:—

"THE MIRROVR OF POLICIE. A Worke no lesse profitable than necessarie, for all Magistrates, and Gouernours of Estates and Commonweales." (Emblematical device of scales, with a serpent in one dish outweighing a cat in the other; the scales are surmounted by a bird's head crowned, and around the whole runs the motto "QVIBVS RESPVBLICA CONSERVETVR.") "LONDON. Printed by Adam Islip. 1598." Colophon. Finis.

4to vol. measuring 1.9 decimetres by 1.43; or 7.48 Eng. inches by 5.63; full pages 1.65 d. by .87; the tree devices about 1.4 d. by .95.
Register. ¶ in 2, *A*—Ll iij in 4s = 136 leaves, all unnumbered.
Contents. ¶ij, the Printer to the Reader. *A*—Ll iij, "The Mirrovr of Policie."

The work is divided into a series of trees, each having a root, from which the branches spring. Of the trees there are *seventeen*, and the nature of the subjects represented by them may be perceived from two or three:—

A ij *verso*. "The three kinds of a good Commonweale:—

Best of al.	Better.	Good.
A kingdome.	The power of the best men.	The power of such as are meanly rich.
Regnum.	*Optimorū potestas*.	*Censu potestas*.
Βασιλεῖα.	Αριστοκρατια.	Τιμοκρατια."

Ff ij. "*The true fashion and image of every good Commonweale.*

	Priests		Sacrifices.
	Magistrates		Judgements.
The	Nobility	for	Armies.
	Citizens		Riches.
	Artificers		Handicraft.
	Husbandmen		Food."

On Ff are the figures of these six orders surrounding a heart in the centre, within which is placed a fortified city. The same figures are also given separately, each followed by a description of the nature of his office or calling.

Kk ij *verso* and Kk iij. "In euerie Countriman that will be called a good Husbandman, are three things required, To know the nature of the ground, and the seasons to sow and reape; Ability to haue oxen, horses, and other instruments for tillage. A will, to be diligent and carefull to perseuer in his country labour."

It is previous to the close of the sixteenth century that we should assign the date of a manuscript Emblem-book which until lately was in the celebrated Corser collection, and which bears the title of—

"CROSSE HIS COVERT, or a Prosopopœicall Treatise: Wherein yᵉ whole course, and condition of his fore pointed time vnto the full Periòde of this his declininge age is ioyntlie deciphered geveing to vnderstande how younge Novices shoulde bestowe the floweringe Pride of there youthfull yeares and greene budding daies in Heroicall exercises, for yᵉ advauncement of theire Countrie, and the assistaunce of theire friendes, and not vnadvisedlie to trace withe wearisome waye and labour some Laberinthe of worldlie vanities, continuallie weavinge the webb of theire owne woe."

The volume is a quarto of 46 pages, and its measurements are 2.02 *decimetres* by 1.48, or 7.95 *Eng. inches* by 5.82. The Emblems consist of 44 stanzas of nine lines each, interspersed with 70 very neatly-drawn devices and 50 shields. Some of the devices are copied from Whitney's *Emblems;* as at p. 16, *Et vsque ad nvbes Veritas;* p. 40, *Icarvs;* p. 42, *Bacchvs;* p. 44, *Occasion*, which may be regarded as the colophon.

Merchant-Taylors' School, established about 1560, is alluded to "as a famous schoole" founded "by famous citizens"; and its first master, Richard Mulcaster, has very honourable mention:

"To traine up youthe in tongues few might compare
With Mulcaster, whose fame shall never fade."

The royal arms, p. 33, are those of Elizabeth and of the Tudors; and the reference to the Belgian Dames, pp. 2-6, agrees with her reign rather than with any other period. Remarks against popery, p. 16, and various leanings to the early Puritans, as p. 17, testify to the same conclusion. The work opens in this way:—

"When Titans fominge steades had girted rounde
The Tropicks Orbe, that bendes to Northen beare:
Before such time, at rage of Sierian hounde
Incensd with heate, had caus'd the Lyon teare."

Of the various Emblem-books for which the world was indebted to Otho Vænius, or rather to his designs and drawings, but one contains an English version;* it is AMORVM EMBLEMATA, Emblemes of Love, *with verses* in *Latin, English, and Italian.* Antverpiæ, obl. 4to. M.DCIIX. Of the Devices there are 125, excellent etchings rather than finished engravings. From the English version we select one as a specimen: FINIS CORONAT OPVS, *Where the end is good, all is good.*

> "The ship toste by the waues doth to no purpose saile,
> Vnlesse the porte shee gayn whereto her course doth tend,
> Right so th' euent of love appeereth in the end,
> For losse it is to loue and neuer to preuaile."

The whole work is dedicated "To the moste honorable and woerthie brothers *William* Earle of *Pembroke*, and *Philip* Earle of *Mountgomerie*, patrons of learning and cheualrie." Of these worthy brothers, *William* appears in the *Mirrovr of Maiestie* as "the Lord Chamberline," p. 22, and *Philip* under his own title, as "Earle of Mountgomerie," p. 34.

A celebrated work, first published in folio in 1610, was John Guillim's DISPLAY OF HERALDRY, pp. 284; it is dedicated "to his most sacred Maiestie," and attained to great celebrity. The sixth edition was published in 1724. Its author, born in Herefordshire in 1565, and dying in 1621, was educated at Brasenose College, Oxford; he afterwards was a member of the Herald's College, and in 1617 was appointed *rouge-croix* pursuivant of arms. Some have attributed the work to Dr. John Barkham, a native of Exeter, who died rector and dean of Bocking, and who was highly regarded for "learning, virtue, and courtesy"; but the point is a doubtful one.

Henry Peacham, the son of a father and author of the same names, who in 1577 published *The Garden of Eloquence,* was schoolmaster at Wymondham, and besides a variety of works, of which Hazlitt's *Hand-Book,* pp. 448-49,

* Hazlitt's *Hand-Book*, p. 624, says: "The English verses are by Richard Verstegan."

enumerates twenty, sent forth a large 4to in 1612, which is strictly a book of Emblems; "MINERVA BRITANNA, or a Garden of Heroicall Deuises, furnished and adorned with *Emblemes* and *Impresa's* of sundry natures." The volume, to which Whitney seems to have furnished the model, numbers 232 pages, in two parts. The Emblems and Devices are 203; to each there is a motto,—to many a dedication, as to the king, princes, and nobles. It has one new feature as a book of Emblems, in the anagrams of names to the honour of which certain devices are devoted; as p. 14, ELISABETHA STEUARTA, which contains the letters out of which may be formed the sentence, *Has Artes beata valet.*

Henry Prince of Wales is the great hero of the book; but as kings and the chief officers of state are freely introduced, it is almost as truly a *Glasse for Royaltie* as the work by H. G. is a *Mirrovr of Maiestie*. From the plates which will be given at the end of our volume of all the Emblems by Peacham which name the same personages, the opportunity will be given for comparing the two works together,—the *Minerva Britanna*, however, being by far the more recondite and learned.

Peacham, in his Address *to the Reader*, speaks of "the many and almost vnimitable *Impresa's* of our owne Countrie: as those of *Edward* the black Prince, *Henry* the fourth, *Henry* the seuenth, *Henry* the eight, Sir *Thomas More*, the Lord *Cromwell*, and of later times, those done by Sir *Phillip* Sidney* and others." And in the *Author's Conclusion* a vision is narrated by him in very readable stanzas of the EMPRESSE OF THE ISLES.

"While proudly vnderfoote she trod
Rich Trophœies, and victorious spoiles."

And with proud boastfulness the writer says—

* So, as quoted in Hazlitt's *Hand-Book*, p. 448, Peacham, in his *Compleat Gentleman*, 1622, remarks "The last [Emblems] I have seen have been the devices of tilting, whereof many were till late reserved in the private gallery at Whitehall, of Sir Philip Sidney, the Earl of Cumberland, Sir Henry Leigh, the Earl of Essex, with many others, most of which I once collected with intent to publish them, but the charge dissuaded me."

> "Here saw I many a shiver'd launce,
> Swordes, Battle-axes, Cannons, Slinges,
> With the armes of *Portvgal* and *Fraunce*,
> And Crownets of her pettie Kinges.
> High-feathered Helmets for the Tilt,
> Bowes, Steelie Targets cleft in twaine;
> Coates, Cornets, Armours richly gilt,
> With tattered Ensignes out of *Spaine*,
> About her now on every Tree,
> (Whereon full oft she cast her eie,)
> Hung silver Sheildes, by three and three,
> With Pen all limned curiouslie :
> Wherein were drawne with skilfull tuch,
> *Impresa's* and *Devises* rare,
> Of all her gallant Knightes, and such
> As Actors in her Conquestes were."

He passes through the splendid roll of names, a true *Mirror of most illustrious men*, from "Great EDVVARD third," and "valiant IOHN of LANCASTER," down to "Couragious ORMOND, LISLE, and SAY," and demands—

> "where may be found,
> These Patrones now of Chivalry."

The whole subject concludes with the assurance—

> "Now what they were, on every Tree
> *Devises* new, as well as old,
> Of those brave worthies, faithfullie,
> Shall in another Booke be told."

Which of Peacham's after-works, if any, may claim to be that "another Booke" does not appear : but about his "*Graphice, or the Most Auncient and Excellent Art of Drawing and Limning*," 4to, 1612, there is an emblematical character ; and also about "THE GENTLEMAN'S EXERCISE ; or an Exquisite practise, as well for drawing of all manner of beasts in their true portraitures, as also the making of all kinds of Colours to be used in lymning, painting, &c.," 4to, also 1612. Of a fugitive "POEME *upon the Birth and in Honor of the Hopefull yong Prince Henrie Frederick*, 1615," 4to—14 leaves, Collier's *Bibliographical Catalogue*, ii. 138, declares, "it has no design, but is a rambling laudatory and emblematical composition far from discreditable to Peacham's taste, scholarship and general knowledge." " He certainly has left nothing better behind him."

Belonging to the reign of James I. there is a fragment in manuscript of an English metrical version of the *Emblems of Alciat*. The former owner of this manuscript, the late Joseph Brooks Yates, of Liverpool, assigned this date to it;* but there are internal signs in the MS. of an earlier time, though not earlier than the end of the sixteenth century. The volume is a folio of 91 leaves, each with an emblem, but having no motto, and a device, usually coloured,—the Latin text and the English stanzas. From there being two devices on p. 55, there are 92 emblems. The drawings, though on a larger scale, follow Plantin's edition of Alciat, 1581, or Rapheleng's, 1608. The 79 coloured devices are generally very bright. In Emblem 88, p. 75, *mudd* has *good* for its rhyming word, and suggests that Lancashire was the county where the translator learned his mother-tongue.

One specimen of the English metrical version will here suffice, especially as it is in contemplation to give the whole version in one of the Holbein Society's future publications. The Emblem is numbered CI. in Rapheleng's edition, 1608; p. 90 of the MS.

SCYPHUS NESTORIS.

" This Cupp of ancient Nestor, with
two bottoms here vptake;
Which worke a massy silverne weight
with charges great did make.
The nailes are goulden, round about
foure handled are to holde,
Vpon each handle settled is
A Doue of yellow gould.
No man but aged Nestor could
this statelie pott vplift:
Tell me I pray you by this Cupp
what was old Homers drift.
The Cupp it self of silver made
sets forth the firmament.
The golden nailes vpon the same
the starres do represent.

---

* See *Transactions of the Liverpool Lit. and Phil. Society*, Nov. 5, 1849.

> The Pleiades some think that he
>   by yellow doues did shade;
> ffor greater and the lesser bere
>   the double bosse he made.
> These things old Nestor by long vse
>   did vnderstand full well,
> Strong men make warres but wise is he
>   that course of starres can tell."

By following the current of time, we have now arrived at THE MIRROVR OF MAIESTIE, which is a work of extreme rarity. The Rev. Thomas Corser, Rector of Stand, near Manchester, by whose very kind permission our facsimile imprint was first photographed and then lithographed, at one time considered his copy the only one known that was absolutely perfect, *ab ovo ad mala*, from beginning to end. This he found to be not strictly correct, and himself afterwards described it as "EXTREMELY RARE, if not almost UNIQUE, there being only one other perfect copy known";* but Mr. Carew Hazlitt's very excellent *Hand-Book*, p. 217, enumerates three copies,—*the Bodleian, Mr. Huth's*, and *Mr. Corser's*, which are equally complete. Another edition, or rather another copy with a fresh title-page, is also mentioned, "Printed by William Iones, dwelling in Red Crosse Streete. 1619. 4$^{to.}$ 34 leaves."

As will be observed on examination, there are *thirty-three* "Noble Personages rancked in the Catalogue," "vnto whom the worke is appropriated," and *thirty-three* coats of arms set forth; but as two Emblems are assigned to the king and only one to the three lord chief justices, there are *thirty-two* Emblems with their devices, all having mottoes, excepting that which is appropriated to the Bishop of London.

The garters around the shields show that, including the sovereign himself, there were *twelve* of the noble personages knights of this most noble order. Of the Royal family,

---

* A pencil note in Mr. Corser's copy says, "*Excessively rare*, only two copies known,—this, which is perfect, and another in the White Knight's collection, which had the title reprinted with the date altered to 1619. At the sale of that library in 1819, Pt. 2, 2924, it was bought by Mr. Perry for £18. It was resold at Perry's sale for £17. 17s. to Mr. Heber, and again in Heber's collection in 1834, Pt. 4, 739, for £7. 10s. 0d. to Thorpe."

three members are named; of the Church, one archbishop and three bishops: there are five of the great officers of state, one duke, one marquis, six earls, two lord viscounts, eight bearing the title of lord, and three lord chief justices.

Though some of the devices and mottoes may be referred to other sources,—as *Emb.* 1, the crown and mitre; *Emb.* 3, the phœnix; *Emb.* 12, the armed hand and sword on the fire; and *Emb.* 16, the armed hand wielding thunderbolts,—yet generally they may be regarded as invented or adapted by the author himself. The stanzas for the armorial bearings frequently refer to them, and those which unfold the meanings of the devices are expressly suited to the symbols and signs that have been employed. Occasionally, however, we have to blame some intemperance of language against those to whom the king and the nation were opposed. Twenty of the mottoes are in Latin; and the others, eleven, in Italian.

Considerable skill is manifested both in the designing of the Emblems and in selecting the mottoes. There is also nearly always appropriateness in the verses which set them forth; but their poetic merit does little to enhance their value. Indeed, the very subjects that are treated of—*achievements* or hatchments of arms, heraldic ensigns, the laudatory or the laboriously-concocted verses, the scrolls of proverbial wisdom or of epigrammatic lore—might serve to dull inspiration where it existed and to bring genius itself down to the level of unfrenzied thought. It is only when we have gained some knowledge of the "noble personages that are rancked" within the volume, and have learned something of their lives and characters,—it is only then that we can take an interest in the measured or, as is often the case, in the unmetrical rhymes appended to names, ensigns, and mottoes; and we regard the work as one exponent, among many, of the reign of a king whom his enemies did not fear, nor did his friends heartily love. He was eager for praise, but unable to deserve it.

Yet we must not forget that the *Mirrovr of Maiestie* reflects names of no trifling mark in the history, whether of their age or of their country. The Archbishop of

Canterbury whom it commemorates was George Abbot; the Bishop of London, John King; the Bishops of Winchester and Ely, James Montagu and Launcelot Andrews.

Of great officers of state, the Lord Chancellor was Francis Bacon; the Lord Treasurer, Thomas Howard, Earl of Suffolk; the Lord Privy Seal, Edward Somerset, Earl of Worcester; the Lord Admiral, Charles Howard, Earl of Nottingham; the Lord Chamberlain, William, Earl of Pembroke; and the Lord Chief Justice of the King's Bench, Sir Henry Montagu.

Then, of other noblemen whose names are introduced, Lodowick Stuart, Duke of Richmond and Lennox, was Chamberlain and Admiral of Scotland; Thomas Howard, Earl of Arundel, had travelled through France and Italy, and made the great collection " of the precious relics of antiquity" which bears his name. Of him, too, it is recorded that he possessed " more Holbeins than all the world besides."* The Earl of Southampton was Shakespeare's friend,† Henry Wriothesley, to whom the poet declared, "if your Honour seeme but pleased, I account my selfe highly praised." Robert Devereux, Earl of Essex, who held the chief command in the army of the Parliament, is named among " the Illustrious and Heroyicall Princes" to whose " Eternall Memorie" the 24 leaves of *Honour in its Perfection*, 4to, 1624, are dedicated: the Lord Viscount Lisle was Robert Sidney, the brother of Sir Philip Sidney; and Richard Sackville, Earl of Dorset, was grandson of Thomas Sackville, who died in 1608, aged 82, and whom Aikin's *Mem. of James I.*, vol. i. p. 304, characterizes as " the extraordinary man of genius, who, after affording in his youth the poetical model of Spenser, was in advanced life selected by Queen Elizabeth to succeed to the station of Lord Burleigh."

Now these are names worthy to be reflected from a *Mirrovr of Maiestie*, and lend to the Majesty itself the brightest glories.

* Aikin's *Mem. of Court of James I.*, vol. i. p. 300.
† Grainger, vol. ii. pp. 30, 31.

It is strange, therefore, that a work of such a name, and with characters so celebrated recorded upon its pages, should have passed into oblivion almost as soon as it was published, and should for above two entire centuries obtain not a word of honourable mention. The first to disinter it was Edmund Lodge, in his *Portraits of Illustrious Personages of Great Britain*, vol. iv. p. 10. Lodge was writing the memoir of the Life of Henry Wriothesley, Earl of Southampton, one of the noblemen to whom, as we have mentioned, an Emblem is assigned in the *Mirrovr of Maiestie;* he spoke of the "Mirrovr" as "a book of such extreme rarity that it may be confidently presumed that it now for the first time offers itself to the notice of modern readers. The nature and method of the little work in question, a copy of which, thought to be unique, is in my hands, will be sufficiently explained by the title." . . . " In this collection, under the arms of the Earl of Southampton, which consist of a cross between five sea-gulls, are these lines" (See *Emb.* 14, *printed* 13) :—

> "No storme of troubles, or cold frosts of Friends,
> Which on free *Greatnes*, too too oft, attends,
> Can (by presumption) threaten your free state :
> For these presaging *sea-birds* doe amate
> Presumptuous *Greatnes :* mouing the best mindes,
> By their approach, to feare the future windes
> Of all calamitie, no lesse then they
> Portend to sea-men a tempestuous day :
> Which you foreseeing may beforehand crosse,
> As they doe them, and so prevent the losse."

"On the opposite page to a biform figure of Mars and Mercury encircled with the motto 'in utraque perfectus,' is subjoined the following compliment" :—

> "WHAT coward *Stoicke*, or blunt captaine will
> Dis-like this *Vnion*, or not labour still
> To reconcile the *Arts* and *victory* ?
> Since in themselues Arts have this quality,
> To vanquish errours traine : what other than
> Should loue the Arts, if not a valiant man ?
> Or, how can he resolue to execute,
> That hath not first learn'd to be resolute ?
> If any shall oppose this, or dispute,
> Your great example shall their spite confute."

The very same copy from which, by the great favour of its owner, the Rev. Thomas Corser, our photolith fac-simile reprint was taken, is the one which Lodge thought to be unique, and which was in his hands when he wrote the memoir of Henry Wriothesley. Written in pencil by Mr. Corser, we found within the cover of it the following record :—

"This very fine copy belonged to the late Edmund Lodge, Esq., and is particularly noticed in the Memoir of Henry Earl of Southampton, where he has quoted the metrical lines which accompany his Arms, and those of the Emblem annexed." "From Lodge it was purchased at the sale by Mr. Bent, of the Aldine Chambers, Paternoster-row, for the sum of £13. 10s."

We add, with some degree of pride in the excellence and rarity of our exemplar, that when Mr. Corser's copy was sold by public auction, March 19, 1869, the final bidding was no less a sum than *thirty-six* pounds sterling.

The authorship of the *Mirrovr of Majestie* remains somewhat in doubt, but Mr. W. Carew Hazlitt, in a work which he edited from Mr. Huth's very valuable collections,—*Poetical Miscellanies*,—interprets H. G. to be the ciphers of Sir Henry Goodere, an attendant on King James. In a note at sign. H H *verso*, on *An Elegy* at sign. D D 4, the editor remarks :—

"*Sir H. G.* It is conjectured that these initials belong to *Sir Henry Goodyeer*, whom the editor inclines to regard as the author of a very rare volume of Emblems, *The Mirrour of Majesty*, 1618. Jonson, among his Epistles, has one to Goodyere, and at the end of Drayton's *Legends*, 1596, 8vo., is a sonnet in praise of the author by *H. G. Esquire*."

It depends on the interpretation we give to the elegy in *the Poetical Miscellanies*, whether we assign it to King James's reign, or later; but the lament is probably over the early death of Prince Henry, when the author asks :—

"Will not he think that, by lamenting thus
The leaving of these kingdoms and of us,
We do not to his new-got Kingdom strive,
Where he is crown'd, his fathers both alive ?"

The same notion that Prince Henry has a "a new-got

kingdom," where, if not literally crowned, he lives in blessedness, occurs in the *Mirrovr's* 4th Emblem, p. 7, dedicated to his brother Charles :—

> " When *Peace* (suspecting he would *warre* inferre,)
> Tooke *Henry* hence, to liue aboue with her,
> She bade *Ioue's Bird* returne from 's quicke convoy
> Of *his faire* soule, left in Heav'ns lasting Ioy."

Seth, too, appears to be King James himself, eulogized and glorified. The *Mirrovr*, Embleme 1, celebrates the sovereign as REX ET SACERDOS DEI, *King and Priest of God*, and thus sounds his praise :—

> " Earth can but make a King of earth partaker
> But Knowledge makes him neerest like his maker.
> For man's meere power not built on Wisdomes fort,
> Dos rather pluck downe kingdomes than support
> Perfectly mixt, thus *Power* and *Knowledge* moue
> About thy *just* designes, ensphear'd with *loue;*
> Which (as a glasse) serue neighbour-Kings to see
> How best to follow, though not equall thee."

The *Elegy* speaks of the work of Nature, and assures us,—

> " She made our world, then us ; she made his head ;
> Our sense and motion from his brain were bred :
> And as two great destructions have and must
> Deface and bring to nothing that of dust,
> So our true world, this princes head and brain,
> A wasteful deluge did and fires sustain.
> But as foresight of two such wastes made Seth
> Erect two columns t' outlive that world's death,
> Against that flood and fire, of brick and stone,
> In which he did by his provision
> Preserve from barbarism and ignorance
> Th' ensuing ages, and did re-advance
> All Sciences, which he engraved there,
> So by our Seth's provision have we here
> Two pillars left : where whatsoe'er we prized
> In our lost world is well characterized.
> The list'ning to this sovereign harmony
> Tames my grief's rage. That now as Elegy
> Made at the first for mourning, hath been since
> Employ'd on love, joy, and magnificence ;
> So this particular elegy shall close
> (Meant for my grief for him), with joy for those.
> " SIR H G."

The first trace I have found of the initials H. G. is at the end of a sonnet in Michaell Drayton's *Tragicall legend of Robert duke of Normandy, surnamed Short-thigh,—with the Legend of Matilda the chast.—And the Legend of Piers Gaveston.* London 1596—16⁰·

> "The vision of Matilda
> Methought I saw upon Matildas Tombe,
>   Her wofull ghost, which Fame did now awake,
> And cr—'d her passage frō Earth's hollow Wombe,
>   To view this Legend, written for her sake:
> No sooner shee her Sacred Name had seene,
> Whom her kind friend had chose to grace his story,
> But wiping her chast teares from her sad eyne,
> She seem'd to tryumph, in her double glory.
>   Glory shee might, that his admired Muse,
> Had with such method fram'd her just complaint:
> But proud she was, that reason made him chuse,
> To patronize the same to such a Saint:
>   In whom her rarest Vertues may be shown
>   Though Poets skil shold faile to make thē known.
>   "H. G. ESQUIRE."

In a description on Latin rhymes by Ralph Calphut (Thomas Cariat), of Brasenose College, Oxford, of "a philosophical feast" there, Sep. 2, 1611, among the guests named as present are Sir Henry Goodere, John West, Hugh Holland, and Inigo Jones."*

Among his other works, the device to which was a duck, with the motto *Non altum peto*, Drayton's *Odes, with other Lyrick Poesies*, were published in folio in 1619, the year after the *Mirrovr of Maiestie*. The Odes bear this dedication, pp. 277–8:—

"TO THE WORTHY KNIGHT AND MY NOBLE FRIEND, SIR HENRY GOODERE, a Gentleman of his Maiesties Priuie Chamber."

> "THESE *Lyrick* Pieces, short, and few,
>   Most worthy Sir, I send to you,
>   To reade them, be not wearie:
>   They may become JOHN HEWES his Lyre,
>   Which oft at *Powlsworth* by the fire
>   Hath made vs grauely merry.

---

* See Mrs. Everett Green's *Calendar of State Papers*, Domestic Series, 1611—1618.

> "Belieue it, he must have the Trick
>   Of Ryming, with Inuention quick,
>   That should due *Lyricks* well :
>   But how I haue done in this kind,
>   Though in my selfe I cannot find,
>   Your Iudgement best can tell.
>
> "Th' old *British* BARDS, vpon their Harpes,
>   For falling Flatts, and rising Sharpes,
>   That curiously were strung ;
>   To stirre their Youth to Warlike Rage,
>   Or their wyld Furie to asswage,
>   In these loose Numbers sung.
>
> "No more I for Fooles Censures passe,
>   Then for the braying of an Asse,
>   Nor once mine Eare will lend them :
>   If you but please to take in gree
>   These *Odes*, sufficient 'tis to mee :
>   Your liking can commend them.
>   "Yours
>   "MICH. DRAYTON."

Out of these materials, I believe, we are not able to construct absolute conviction. But whether Sir Henry Goodere be the author or not, certain it is that the initials H. G. were attached to the original *Mirrovr of Maiestie* in 1618 ; and now, in 1870, this introductory notice of a fac-simile reprint is signed with the same monogram. The *metempsychoses* for 250 years, through at least *seven* generations, from the author to the editor, I leave to be explained by some one who, like Joseph Glanvill, an early defender of the Royal Society of England, affirms,—

"The sages of old live again in us." "We are our re-animated ancestours, and antedate their resurrection."

H. G.

II.

ANNOTATIONS ON THE ARMORIAL BEARINGS AND NOBLE PERSONAGES.

HERALDRY, in its expressive symbolism embodying a wide range of thought in the visible form of a simple image, speaks the same language as Emblems—possessing many features in common and oftentimes so closely interwoven as scarcely to be distinguishable, it ought rather to be considered as a branch of the same subject than a distinct science. Each speaks laconically to the mind through the eye, by the agency of figurative imagery conveying distinctive ideas, and both seem to have had their origin in that love of symbolical expression which in the rudest conditions of barbarism not less than in the most advanced stages of civilization has been one of the component elements of the human mind.

The two extremes of the human family seem almost to stand side by side in their adoption of this heraldic symbolism; indeed nature had hardly imparted to man the instinct of self-preservation when he found it necessary to impress some device or cognizance upon his own tribe, that he might distinguish it from those which were inimical to him. Our knowledge of the habits of barbarous nations leads to the conclusion that in the most primitive stages of society the chiefs of different tribes, in the ignorance of written language, adopted some such emblematic devices as would convey in the simplest manner an idea of their predominant qualities or peculiar characteristics. Symbolical figures are known to have been emblazoned upon the

F

standards of the Egyptians and Assyrians. Diodorus Siculus affirms that the former nation was the first to adopt these military ensigns, and that the animals borne thereon afterwards came to be worshipped as deities. Of their early use there can be no doubt, for several Rabbinical writers assert that their history affords abundant proof that such distinctive devices were in use among the Egyptians previous to the departure of the Israelites from their land. That the Israelites themselves had their distinctive blazonry, we have the testimony of Holy Writ:— "Every man of the children of Israel shall pitch by his own standard, with the ensign of their father's house : far off about the tabernacle of the congregation shall they pitch";* and we might also notice the arguments that have been advanced to prove that the same semi-mystic symbolism prevailed among the nations springing from the Scythians, the Medes and Persians, and others.

Nearly five hundred years before the Christian era, the Greek tragedian Æschylus described with minute exactness the heraldic insignia of the chieftains who united their forces for the siege of Thebes before the Trojan war. In Europe, a personal symbolism may be traced almost from the first dawn of historical tradition, and there is abundant evidence to show that a similar usage prevailed among the races that peopled the valley of the Nile. The uncivilized tribes inhabiting the Far West possess a faint glimmering of the science, and the same expressive symbolism is found among the aboriginal chiefs of Australia. The owl was the distinctive cognizance of the Athenians, as the eagle was of the polished subjects of the Cæsars; and in like manner the wolf's head was the crest of Argos, and the tortoise of the Peloponnesus, whilst the winged dragon has ever presided over the heraldry of the Chinese.

The shield, as the most important piece of defensive armour, by the aid of the limner became also the medium of recognition among friends; and hence it was almost invariably embellished with some distinctive personal cognizance supposed to typify the peculiar characteristics of the

* Numbers ii. 2.

owner, or to illustrate some remarkable feat or martial exploit in which he might have been engaged. It is affirmed that armorial distinctions were first used by Anubis and Macedo, sons of Osiris, under the emblems of a wolf and a dog. Both the Greeks and Romans emblazoned their shields with such devices; and in the writings of Livy we find how frequently individual soldiers received a cognomen in commemoration of some notable incident or heroic action; and what more likely than that the cognomen should suggest the personal cognizance. One instance may be mentioned. A Gaul having challenged to single combat any one of the Roman army, a tribune of the soldiers, Marcus Valerius, demanded permission from the consul to accept it. This having been granted, the Roman volunteer advanced against his enemy and slew him, when, to commemorate the circumstance of a raven having lighted upon his helmet and attacked the face and eyes of the Gaul as the conflict proceeded, the victorious tribune assumed the additional name of *Corvinus*, and bore a raven in the act of assault for crest upon his helmet, which was afterwards continued by his successors.

Advancing imperceptibly in the train of civilization, these personal signs and emblematic devices which from the very earliest periods had almost universally prevailed, assumed a distinct form and became subject to certain laws, and thus gradually an organized system of Heraldry arose, which had its full development in the Middle Ages, when it constituted an hereditary mark of honour, " authorized by sovereigns for distinguishing, differencing, and illustrating persons, families, and communities."[*]

A kind of Heraldry distinct from the ordinary insignia appears to have been in vogue before the regular adoption of coat-armour, and to have continued in high favour until the reign of Elizabeth, when it gradually fell into disuse, with the other brilliant relics of the feudal system. This was the badge or personal cognizance assumed by families of rank or importance, and used principally for the decoration of costume, military equipments, caparisons, and

* Nisbet.

the liveries of armed followers and retainers. Shakspeare adverts to the use of this mark of identity in the Second Part of King Henry V. (Act V. scene 1), where Clifford concludes his threatening address to Warwick with the words—

> "I am resolved to bear a greater storm
> Than any thou canst conjure up to-day;
> And that I'll write upon thy burgonet,
> Might I but know thee by thy household badge."

The word "household" clearly denoting that the badge was used to distinguish the retainers of the eminent personage to whom it pertained.

In the review of the English Emblem-Books which preceded the Mirrovr of Maiestie, given in the earlier part of this volume, reference is made to the badges adopted by the sovereigns of England. Many of them are enumerated in Burke's *Encyclopædia of Heraldry*, and a very complete list will be found in the Rev. Charles Boutell's *Heraldry Historical and Popular*. One of the earliest, and perhaps the most famous of all, was the sprig of broom. *Plantagenistæ*, the emblem of humility, borne by Geoffrey of Anjou, and assumed by his descendants; whence arose a name immortal in English history—the patronymic of the royal race of the Plantagenets. A favourite badge of Richard II. was the white hart couchant, an emblem derived, no doubt, from that of his mother, Joan of Kent, who bore a white hind couchant under a tree, gorged and chained, *or*. Another renowned historical badge was the falcon and the fetterlock, the cognizance of King Edward IV., respecting the adoption of which the following story is narrated by Dr. Barrington in his *Lectures on Heraldry* (pp. 182-3):—"Edmund of Langley, the great-grandfather of Edward IV., bore for impress 'a faulcon in a fetterlock,' implying that he was shut up from all hope and possibility of the kingdom, when his brother John of Gaunt began to aspire thereto. Whereupon he asked, upon a time when he saw his sons viewing his device set up in a window, what was Latin for a fetterlock? Whereat, when the young gentlemen studied, the father said, 'Well, if you cannot tell me, I will tell you—*Hic hæc hoc taceatis*,' as advising them to be silent and quiet, saying, 'Yet God knows what may come to pass hereafter.' This his great-grandson (Edward IV.) repeated, when he commanded that his younger son, Richard Duke of York, should use this device, with the fetterlock *opened*."

The well-known feather badge has been the device of the Princes of Wales from the time of Arthur, son of Henry VII. The ostrich feathers were held in high esteem by the Black Prince, who gave precise instructions for their display among the armorial achievements to be placed above his tomb. These compositions were to be twelve in number, six being for war—"*de nos armez entiers quartelles*," and the remainder of ostrich feathers for peace,—"*et qe sur chacun escuchon soit escript, c'est assavier sur cellez de noz armez et sur les autres des plumes d'ostruce,—Houmout.*" * The old tradition, which affirms that this device was won at Crescy from the blind king of Bohemia, who perished in the thick of the fight, requires more positive corroboration before it can be accepted as genuine history. The badge of the king of Bohemia was a vulture, and there is certainly no evidence to show that the Black Prince himself ever associated the device with his early exploit at Crescy. The ostrich feathers are first mentioned in 1369 on the plate of Philippa, and were used by all the sons of Edward II., and of all the kings until Arthur Tudor, Prince of Wales, son of Henry VII., first ensigned the three feathers with a coronet, since which they have been appropriated to the Princes of Wales.

Shakspeare makes frequent allusion to the Cognizances —the sun† and the boar—borne by the two brothers of

---

* It is worthy of note that the Black Prince's tomb in Canterbury Cathedral presents a perplexing discrepancy from the letter of his will. The escutcheons of arms are actually surmounted by labels inscribed "*houmout*," whilst those with ostrich feathers have the motto "*ich diene*," not mentioned in the Prince's injunctions.

† The "sun in splendour" was adopted as an heraldic cognizance by Edward IV., in memory, as we are told, "of the three suns" which are said to have appeared in the heavens when he gained the victory over the Lancastrians at the battle of Mortimer's Cross.

the House of York, Edward IV. and Richard III.; as, for instance :—

> "Now is the winter of our discontent
> Made glorious summer by the *sun* of York."
> *King Richard III.*, Act I. sc. 1.

And—

> "To fly the boar before the boar pursues,
> Were to incense the boar to follow us,
> And make pursuit, where he did mean no chase.
> Go, bid thy master rise and come to me;
> And we will both together to the Tower,
> Where, he shall see, the boar will use us kindly."
> *King Richard III.*, Act III. sc. 2.

The last-named cognizance being also commemorated in the whimsical *jeu d'esprit* which cost the author, William Collingbourne, his life :—

> "The Rat, the Cat, and Lovel the dog,
> Rule all England under a Hog."

The couplet having allusion to the names of the two royal favourites, Ratcliffe and Catesby, to the crest of Lord Lovel, which was a dog, and the boar, the cognizance of Richard III.

Not less famous was the cognizance of the Nevilles:—

> "The rampant bear chained to the ragged staff,"

which was borne both as a crest and badge, and is thus referred to by Shakspeare in the Second Part of King Henry VI. (Act v. sc. 1), when York, after being charged as a traitor by Lord Clifford, replies :—

> "Look in a glass, and call thy image so;
> I am thy king, and thou a false-heart traitor,—
> Call hither to the stake my two brave bears,
> That with the very shaking of their chains
> They may astonish these fell-lurking curs :
> Bid Salisbury and Warwick come to me."

It was not until the long reign of Henry III. that heraldic blazonry first assumed a systematic character and its hereditary use became established, arms having previously been assumed at will as military ensigns, and then adopted as honourable distinctions. That great military enterprise which leagued together the chivalry of Europe —the Crusades—necessitated a more definite system of military insignia than had previously been prevalent. Each warrior of rank adopted some recognized device or composition, which was displayed upon his knightly pennon and banner, and emblazoned upon the shield and the rich surcoat which he wore over his armour; and modifications of these devices would, of necessity, be assigned to his followers ; and hence the names, *coats of arms* and *coat armour*. In this way armorial bearings took their rise, and also became subject to certain laws, which protected the bearer in the exclusive use of them. At this period the cross became a very common bearing among the Crusaders,* and pilgrims afterwards adopted it as their cognizance.

> " A bloodie cross he bore,
> The dear remembrance of his dying Lord,
>   For whose sweet sake that glorious badge he wore.
> And dead, as living, ever Him adored :
> Upon his shield the like was also scored."

In the Crusade confederacy, the practical utility of heraldry was felt and appreciated; its popularity increased during the fierce social struggle of the Roses, and its reputation was maintained until the accession of the Tudors, when its decline may be said to have begun, along with that social system in which it had its origin.

Though in ancient times arms were voluntarily assumed, they were also frequently granted by the sovereign as honourable distinctions to those who were of "gentle" descent or had signalized themselves in tournament or battle ; and hence they became the avowed marks of honour, gentility, and family distinction : an eager desire for their possession was manifested by all who had interest

---

* Mackenzie says that in the Crusades, the English carried a cross, *or ;* the Scotch, a St. Andrew's cross *;* the French, a cross, *argent ;* the Germans, *sable ;* the Italians, *azure ;* and the Spaniards, *gules.*

in the soil, whether they had served in any military capacity or not, and great pride was taken in their display.

"Although arms," says an heraldic writer, "were, in their first acceptation, taken up at any gentleman's pleasure, yet hath that liberty for many ages been deny'd, and they, by regal authority, made the rewards and ensigns of merit, or the gracious favours of princes; no one being, by the law of gentility in England, allowed the bearing thereof but those that either have them by descent or grant. Therefore Henry V., by proclamation, did inhibit thus:—'*Quod nullus cujuscunque status, gradus seu conditionis fuerit, hujusmodi arma sive tunicas armorum in se sumat, nisi ipse jure antecessorio vel ex donatione alicujus ad hoc sufficientem potestatem habentis, ea possideat aut possidere debeat, et quod ipse arma sive tunicas illas ex cujus dono obtinet, demonstrationis suæ personis ad hoc per nos assignatis seu assignandis manifeste demonstret, exceptis illis que nobiscum apud bellum de Agincourt arma portabant,*'" &c. And the great legal luminary, the Lord Chief Justice Coke, affirmed that every gentleman must be "*arma gerens*," and that the best test of gentle blood is the bearing of arms.

That being so, it was natural that a work like the one now reproduced, which, not by speech or outward expression, but through the agency of an ideal symbolism, professed to shadow forth the distinguishing qualities and personal virtues of the illustrious individuals represented, should also give those avowed and recognized evidences of hereditary rank and honourable distinction embodied in their heraldic insignia, and thus extend and intensify its own poetic imagery by means of accumulative association.

Having sketched thus hastily the rise and progress of Heraldic blazonry under its variously modified forms, we proceed to notice briefly the several "Noble Personages rancked in the Catalogue," "vnto whom the worke is appropriated."

J. C.

THE KING, pp. 1—3.

ARMS.—Quarterly :—1st and 4th Grand Quarters, Quarterly, 1st and 4th, *az.*,* three fleurs-de-lys, two and one, *or*, for France Modern ;† 2nd and 3rd, *gu.*, three lions passant guardant, in pale, *or*, for England. 2nd Grand Quarter, *or*, a lion rampant, *gu.*, within a double tressure, fleurie counter fleurie, for Scotland. 3rd Grand Quarter, *az.*, a harp, *or*, stringed, *az.*, for Ireland. The shield encircled by a garter inscribed with the motto of the order, *Honi soit qui mal y pense*, and ensigned with a crown and the initials I.R.

James the First of England and the Sixth of Scotland was the only son of Mary Queen of Scots, by Henry Stuart, Lord Darnley, and great-grandson of Margaret, elder daughter of Henry VII. of England. He was born at Edinburgh Castle, June 19, 1566, and baptized according to the rites of the Catholic Church in Stirling Castle, by the names of Charles James, December 17th following; his sponsors being Charles IX. of France, Philibert Duke of Savoy, and Elizabeth of England, the latter sending as a gift to her godson a golden font valued at three thousand crowns.

On the death of Elizabeth, March 24, 1603, James succeeded as direct heir to the crown of England, although expressly excluded by the statutes in force, which vested the legal right to the throne in Lord Seymour, eldest son of the Earl of Hereford, by Lady Katharine Grey (sister of Lady Jane Grey), as heir of Mary, Duchess of Suffolk,

---

* In the *Mirrovr*, the arms are in every instance depicted in outline only, without any indication of tincture, an omission it has been thought desirable to supply.

† Charles V. of France, with a view apparently to distinguish between his own arms and the fleurs-de-lys borne by the English claimants of his crown, reduced the number of his fleurs-de-lys to *three* only. The same change was effected by Heury IV. in the 1st and 4th Quarters of the Arms of England; and impressions of his Great Seal, taken in the years 1406 and 1409, exist, which bear the quartered arms (on banners instead of shields) charged with three fleurs-de-lys only. This modification of the French shield, which bears three fleurs-de-lys only, is styled in Heraldry " France Modern "; and thus is distinguished from the shield semée de lys, *or*, "France Ancient."— BOUTELL.

younger sister of Henry VIII. He was proclaimed at Whitehall and Cheapside on the day following Elizabeth's decease, the popular voice being undoubtedly raised in his favour, in consequence of a natural opinion that he was the lawful heir, though his hereditary pretensions were not acknowledged and ratified by Parliament until March, 1604.* On receiving intelligence of Elizabeth's death, he at once proceeded to London, and was crowned with his queen, Anne of Denmark, at Westminster, July 25, 1603.

King James was seized with a tertian ague at Theobalds, near Cheshunt, where he died on Sunday, the 27th March, 1625, in the fifty-ninth year of his age, and after a reign over England of twenty-two years, and was succeeded by his only surviving son, Charles, Prince of Wales, his eldest son, the Prince Henry, having pre-deceased him.

In the character of James there is little to command respect or create esteem: weak, vain, and pedantic, he lacked those nobler qualities which go to the making of a great man or an illustrious king. As a sovereign his character may be briefly summed up in the remark that he reigned like a woman, after a woman who had reigned like a man.

THE QVEENE, pp. 4, 5.

ARMS.—On a lozenge, a cross *gu.*, surmounted of another *arg*. In the dexter canton, *or*, semée of hearts ppr., three lions passant guardant, in pale, *az.*, crowned *or*, for Denmark; in the sinister canton, *gu.*, a lion rampant, crowned *or*, holding in his paws a battle-axe *arg.*, for Norway; in the dexter base quarter, *az.*, three crowns ppr., for Sweden; and in the sinister base quarter, *or*, semée of hearts, *gu.*, in chief a lion passant guardant *az.*, for Jutland. In the base of the lozenge, beneath the cross, the ancient ensign of the Vandals, *gu.*, a wyvern, its tail nowed and wings expanded, *or*. Upon the centre of the cross, an

* 1 Jac. I. c. 1.

escutcheon of pretence charged with quarterly, first, *or*, two lions passant guardant *az.*, for Sleswick; second, *gu.*, an inescutcheon, having a nail in every point thereof, in triangle, between as many holly-leaves, all ppr., for Holstein; third, *gu.*, a swan *arg.*, beaked *sa.*, gorged with a coronet ppr., for Stormerk; and fourth, *az.*, a chevalier armed at all points, brandishing his sword, his helm plumed, his charger *arg.*, the trappings *or*, for Ditzmers. Over the whole on an inescutcheon *az.*, a cross patée fitchée *or*, for Dalmenhurst, impaling for Oldenburgh, *or*, two bars *gu.* The whole ensigned with a crown.*

The lady by whom this complicated example of the elaboration of heraldic details was borne—Anne, princess of Denmark, queen of James I., was the second daughter of Frederick II., king of Denmark and Norway, by Sophia, daughter of the duke of Mecklenburg. She was born at Scanderburg, December 12, 1575, and educated as a zealous Protestant of the Lutheran creed. Her father was accounted one of the richest sovereigns in Europe; and, as a prudent prince, had accumulated large dowries for his daughters, whose hands were sought by many of the northern princes. Her marriage with James took place by proxy at the Danish court, on the 20th of August, 1589, she being then in her fourteenth year. The king having learned that his bride would be unable to reach Scotland until the following spring, resolved on a journey to Norway, where her vessel had taken shelter, in order to meet her. He embarked at Leith on the 19th October, accompanied by four other vessels, and landed at Slaikray, in Norway, whence he proceeded, partly by land and partly by sea, to Upslo, where the queen was staying, arriving there on the 19th November. The marriage was celebrated on the Sunday following, Mr. David Lyndsay, the king's own minister, performing the nuptial ceremony in the French language. On the

---

* These arms are identical with those borne by Frederick II., father of the Queen Consort, who was elected a Knight of the Garter in 1578, as appears by the blazonry in his stall-plate, which is still preserved at Windsor.

1st of May, 1590, the king and queen landed at Leith, and thence proceeded to Edinburgh, where, on the 17th of the same month, she was crowned in the abbey church of Holyrood. As dower, James received with his bride the islands of Orkney and Shetland, which had in the preceding century been pawned by Denmark to Scotland; and thus he completed the geographical wholeness of his inheritance.

On his accession to the throne of England in 1603, Anne became the first queen-consort of Great Britain, a title which has been borne by the wives of our sovereigns from that time to the present. Her death occurred at Hampton Court on Tuesday, the 2nd March, 1619; and on the following Tuesday her body was conveyed to Denmark House, in the Strand, where it lay in state until the 13th May, when it was buried in Westminster Abbey. Her hearse, which remained standing over the place of her interment the whole of the reign of James I., was destroyed during the civil wars, with many a funeral memento of more durable materials. In addition to her eldest son, Henry Prince of Wales, who died in 1612, in his eighteenth year, she had issue Robert, Margaret, and Sophia, who died young; Charles, afterwards Charles I., and Elizabeth, married to Frederick V., duke of Bavaria, Elector Palatine of the Rhine, and king of Bohemia, both of them singularly unfortunate.

Many tributes in verse were offered to her memory, and Camden has preserved two elegiac epitaphs, one of which possesses some elegance of thought :—

> "March, with his winds, hath struck a cedar tall,
> And weeping April mourns that cedar's fall;
> And May intends no flowers her month shall bring,
> Since she must lose the flower of all the spring :
> Thus March's winds hath caused April's showers,
> And yet sad May must lose her flower of flowers."*

Another, written by King James himself, which contains an allusion to the comet supposed to have foreboded the queen's death, is very characteristic of the royal author :—

* Camden's Remains, 397.

ARMS AND PERSONAGES.

> " Then to invite the great God sent a star;
> His nearest friend and kin good princes are,
> Who, though they run their race of man and die,
> Death serves but to refine their majesty.
> So did my queen her court from hence remove,
> And left the earth to be enthroned above;
> Then she is changed, not dead,—no good prince dies,
> But like the sun, doth only set to rise." *

THE PRINCE, pp. 6, 7.

In the plate assigned to Prince Charles we have the ordinary feather badge of the princes of Wales, to which allusion has already been made †—A plume of ostrich feathers, *arg.*, quilled, *or;* enfoiled with a prince's coronet of the last, with an escroll, *az.*, thereon the words *Ich Dien*.

The Prince Charles, son of James I. by his Queen Anne of Denmark, was born at Dunfermline, in Scotland, November 19, 1600; and after the death of his elder brother, Prince Henry, in 1612, was created Prince of Wales in 1616.‡ Subsequently negotiations were entered into with the Court at Madrid for a marriage with the prince and the Infanta of Spain; but these were conducted in such a manner that five years elapsed without the treaty being brought to any conclusion; and in 1623 Charles, attended by the profligate minister Buckingham, proceeded to Spain to conclude it in person. On his way he visited Paris, where he saw for the first time the Princess Henrietta Maria, daughter of Henry IV. of France, who was destined to exercise so great an influence over him. Charles with his attendant reached Madrid, and the articles were so far settled, that it was expected the union would be celebrated in the same year; but through the influence of Buckingham the match was eventually broken off, and an alliance was soon after concluded with Henrietta Maria.

---

* Cole's MSS.   † Vide *ante*, p. 101.   ‡ Granger, ii. 237.

On the death of King James in 1625, Charles ascended the throne, and on Candlemas-day of the same year he was crowned at Westminster. Before he had solemnized the funeral of his father, his marriage with Henrietta Maria of France was concluded; and on the 1st May, 1625, it was solemnized at Paris, the Duke de Chevreuse acting as proxy; after which the queen set out for her husband's court, attended by Buckingham, and arrived at Dover on the 13th June, where she was received by Charles.

A record of the events which marked the troublesome and unfortunate reign of Charles does not come within the scope of these brief notes. The king had inherited from his father inordinate notions of kingly power, and resolutely shut his eyes to the fact that the influence of the people had increased, and that he had to deal with an entirely different state of public opinion. Persistent in his determination to reign and govern by "divine right," he refused to yield anything, and in the fierce struggle which he provoked he fell. In December, 1648, the Commons resolved that he should be tried on the charge of treason in making war on his Parliament, and a special "High Court of Justiciary," which had no authority in the English constitution, was formed. Before this tribunal, which assembled in Westminster Hall, Charles was brought. On the 27th January, 1649, sentence was pronounced against him, and on the 30th he was beheaded in front of Whitehall, his last words to Bishop Juxon, who attended him, being to charge the Prince Charles, his son, to forgive his father's murderers.

Charles had issue by his queen, Henrietta Maria, Charles, Prince of Wales, who succeeded as Charles II.; James, Duke of York, who succeeded his elder brother as James II.; Henry, Duke of Gloucester, who died unmarried in 1660; and Mary, espoused to William II., Prince of Orange, by whom she had an only son, William Henry, who ascended the British throne as William III.; and four other children.

THE ARCH-BISHOP OF CANTERBVRY, pp. 8, 9.

ARMS.—*Az.*, an archiepiscopal staff, in pale, *or*, ensigned with a cross patée *arg.*, surmounted by a pall of the last, fimbriated and fringed gold, and charged with four crosses formées fitchées *sa.*; the arms of the See of Canterbury impaling, *gu.*, a chevron between three pears, pendent, stalked, *or*, for Abbot.*

George Abbot, Archbishop of Canterbury, whose arms are above described, was born of humble parentage, his father being a weaver and cloth-worker (or, according to some accounts, a clock-maker) at Guildford, in Surrey, in which town the prelate first saw the light in 1562.† He received his early education in the Grammar-school of his native place, and removed thence to Baliol College, Oxford. Afterwards he became successively Master of University College, Dean of Winchester, and Vice-Chancellor of Oxford, and eventually he was raised to the See of Lichfield and Coventry; thence he was translated to London; and, lastly, he was selected to succeed Richard Bancroft as Archbishop of Canterbury; installed at Lambeth on Tuesday, April 9, 1611, and sworn a Privy Councillor at Greenwich on the 23rd June following.

Archbishop Abbot was a firm Protestant and a zealous and powerful leader of the Puritanical party, and as such a determined opponent of Laud, whose policy he resisted with uncompromising resolution. A stern moralist, he had disapproved of the *Book of Sports*, and boldly forbade its being read in his church at Croydon; and he openly remonstrated against the articles of the proposed Spanish marriage, which had given great offence to the

---

* The arms of the Archbishop may still be seen at Canterbury and at Guildford.
† The house in which Archbishop Abbot was born remained standing until July, 1863.

Protestant feeling of England. At one time Abbot was distinguished for his rigorous maintenance of the doctrines of divine right and passive obedience; but, after the accession of Charles I., whom he crowned at Westminster, his views changed, and he became an equally resolute opponent of the despotic measures of the king, and peremptorily refused to license a sermon dedicated to his majesty, in which the preacher, Dr. Sibthorpe, asserted that the king was not himself bound to observe the laws of the realm, but that his subjects were bound to obey him in whatever might be his commands.

In 1623, being with a hunting party at the seat of Lord Zouch, in Hampshire, he had the misfortune to shoot one of his lordship's keepers, an act of casual homicide that caused his retirement for a time, during which he resided at his country residence near Croydon. He died at Croydon in 1633, and was buried at Guildford, in which town he had founded and liberally endowed a hospital for poor men and women, and where his tomb still remains.

Though lowly-born, the Abbot family contained the elements of greatness. Robert, the elder brother of the Archbishop, became Bishop of Salisbury, and another brother filled the office of Lord Mayor of London. Fuller speaks of the three as "a happy ternion of brothers." "George" he describes "as the more plausible preacher, Robert the greatest scholar; George the abler statesman, Robert the deeper divine; gravity," he adds, "did frown in George, and smile in Robert." Clarendon, who has furnished us with portraits of so many public men of the Stuart and Commonwealth periods, describes the Archbishop as "of morose manners and sour aspect." As Dean of Westminster, "he was the second of eight divines to whom the translation of the *whole New Testament* was committed" by order of James l., there being fifty-four translators nominated for the entire Bible now in use.

THE LORD CHANCELLOR, pp. 10, 11.

ARMS.—*Gu.*, on a chief, *arg.*, two mullets pierced, *sa.*, differenced by a crescent, as denoting the younger line.

Francis Bacon, Baron Verulam and Viscount St. Albans, one of the greatest of English philosophers, was the youngest son of Sir Nicholas Bacon, Lord Keeper of the Great Seal, by his wife, one of the daughters of Sir Anthony Cooke, tutor to King Edward VI., and was born at York House, in the Strand, January 22, 1561. At twelve years of age he began his academical career at Trinity College, Cambridge, and such was the progress he made, that at sixteen he had become master of the whole circle of liberal arts as then understood. On quitting the university, he travelled over France, but returned to England on the death of his father in 1579, after which he studied the common law in Gray's Inn, and was called to the bar at the age of twenty-one. In 1593 he entered Parliament, and having written in favour of the union of England and Scotland, he received the honour of knighthood after the accession of James I., July 23, 1603.

Though he had a formidable rival in Sir Edward Coke, Bacon rose rapidly into favour; in 1605 he was appointed to the office of Solicitor-General, and on the 25th October, 1613, he became Attorney-General. On the 9th June, 1616, he was sworn of the Privy Council; on the 7th March following, he was appointed Lord Keeper of the Great Seal; and on the death of Lord Chancellor Ellesmere, a few days later, was named Lord Chancellor of England. On Sunday, July 12, 1618, he was elevated to the peerage by the title of Baron Verulam, and created Viscount St. Albans January 27, 1627.

Bacon had now attained the height of his popularity, and from this time may be dated the beginning of his miserable fall. Complaints were made of his venality as a judge, and the House of Commons having impeached him as being guilty of corruption upon his own confession, he was fined £40,000, deprived of all his offices, and committed to the Tower during the king's pleasure. After a time he was set at liberty and the greater part of the fine remitted, but he remained absent from the court, and continued to live in retirement, devoting his life to those philosophical studies which he had never forgot or neglected, even in the midst of honours or when burdened with the cares of state. When only nineteen, he wrote a *General View of the State of Europe*. His great works are the *Novum Organum* and the *De Augmentis Scientiarum*. The former, projected in his youth, was prefaced by a series of sketches, revised and rewritten, and finally published in 1620. The latter appeared in 1603, and the English edition (*Advancement of Learning*) in 1605. The *Essays* were first published in 1597, but large additions were subsequently made. Among his other works are the *Wisdom of the Ancients, History of Henry VII., Felicities of Queen Elizabeth*, &c. Addison says that he had the sound, distinct, and comprehensive knowledge of Aristotle, with all the beautiful light graces of Cicero; and Lord Orford, who calls him the prophet of the arts which Newton was afterwards to reveal, pronounces that his genius and his works must be universally admired as long as science exists.

He died at the Earl of Arundel's, Highgate, April 9, 1626, and was buried in the chapel of St. Michael's Church, St. Albans, where a monument was erected to his memory by his indefatigable secretary Sir Thomas Meauty.

Lord Bacon married, about the year 1605, Alice, daughter and coheir of Benedict Barham, Esquire, Alderman of London, but never had any issue.

THE LORD TREASVRER, pp. 12, 13.

ARMS.—*Gu.*, a bend between six cross crosslets, fitchée, *arg.*, differenced by a crescent, the mark of cadency of a second son; the shield encircled by a garter, inscribed with the motto of the order, and ensigned with an earl's coronet.

The coat, as above described, is the one known to heralds as "Howard Ancient," being without the "Flodden Augmentation," now borne by the noble house of Howard, and which the Lord Treasurer was entitled to blazon; viz., upon the bend, an escutcheon, *or*, charged with a demi-lion rampant, pierced through the mouth with an arrow, within a double tressure flory, counter-flory, *gu.*, an augmentation of merit granted by Henry VIII. to Thomas Howard, second Duke of Norfolk, and his posterity, for his victory at Flodden Field, wherein King James IV. of Scotland was slain, September 9, 1513.

Thomas Lord Howard, Earl of Suffolk, and Lord High Treasurer of England, was the eldest son by the second marriage of the unfortunate Thomas, fourth Duke of Norfolk, "the most powerful and the most popular man in England," but who, allured by ambition, formed or assented to the ill-judged project for a matrimonial alliance with Mary Queen of Scots, then the captive of the implacable Elizabeth, with the hope of becoming eventually King-Consort of England—a scheme that cost him his life. He was grandson of the famous Earl of Surrey, his mother being Margaret, daughter and heir of Thomas, Lord Audley of Walden.

Lord Howard inherited his mother's estates, and in 27 Elizabeth (1584) was restored in blood by Act of Parliament. In early life he embraced the military service, but afterwards abandoned it for the court, and succeeded in a great measure in obtaining the favour of

Elizabeth. In 1587 he was appointed Vice-Admiral of the Fleet despatched to Cadiz, and the following year he was associated with his kinsman, Lord Charles Howard of Effingham, in the command of the fleet fitted out to oppose the Spanish Armada; and some years later, October 24, 1597, he was summoned to Parliament as Lord Howard of Walden. He was fortunate enough to obtain the favour of King James I., by whom he was much honoured. On the 3rd May, 1603, immediately after his accession, James arrived at Theobalds, in Hertfordshire, the residence of Secretary Cecil; and on the following day Lord Thomas Howard was sworn a Privy Councillor, along with his uncle, Lord Henry Howard, and other noblemen. On the 7th of the same month his majesty entered London, and was entertained at the Charter House by Lord Howard for the space of four days. On the 21st July following he was advanced to the earldom of Suffolk, being the first earl of the king's creation, and installed a Knight of the Garter; and about the same time he was appointed Lord Chamberlain. To his vigilance and sagacity while discharging the duties of this office, the discovery of the "Gunpowder Plot" has been mainly attributed, he having searched the vaults beneath the house on the day before the meeting of Parliament, and there discovered Fawkes preparing for the terrible enterprise. In 1613 the earl was elected Chancellor of the University of Cambridge, and on the 13th July in the following year he was constituted Lord High Treasurer of England. His countess having, unfortunately, gained too great an ascendancy over him, used it in making him a party to her extortions on those who had business to transact at the Treasury; charges of embezzlement were in consequence brought against her husband, which resulted in his being deprived of the office, July 19, 1618; a fine of £30,000 was also inflicted, but which was reduced by the king to £7,000. His death occurred 28th May, 1626.

The high and lucrative offices enjoyed by the earl afforded him ample means for the display of magnificence. During his lifetime he built the stately mansions of Audley End,

ARMS AND PERSONAGES.

in Essex, and Charlton House, in Wiltshire; the former at a cost, as is stated, of £190,000.

The Earl of Suffolk was twice married, his first wife being Mary, sister of Thomas Lord Dacre, of Gillesland, who dying without issue, his lordship married, secondly, Catharine, eldest daughter and coheir of Sir Henry Knevet, knight, of Chalton, co. Wilts, and widow of the Hon. Richard Rich, eldest son of Lord Rich, by whom he had seven sons and three daughters.

THE LORD PRIVY SEALE, pp. 14, 15.

ARMS.—*Arg.* on a fesse, France and England quarterly, within a bordure componée *arg.* and *az.*, encircled by a garter inscribed with the motto of the order and ensigned with the coronet of an earl. Charles Somerset, first Earl of Worcester, bore as an abatement a baton sinister, the mark of illegitimacy, across his quartered arms, couped by the bordure, but his eldest son, Henry, the second earl, removed the baton from his shield, and charged Beaufort upon a fesse on a silver shield, as above described; thus retaining an abatement whilst rejecting the baton.

Edward Somerset, only son of William, third Earl of Worcester, by his wife Christian, daughter of Edward Lord North, of Cathladge, and great-grandson of Charles, the illegitimate son of Henry Beaufort, Duke of Somerset, succeeded as fourth earl on the death of his father, February 22, 1587. In 1590 he was sent on a diplomatic mission to James VI. of Scotland, to congratulate him upon his marriage with the Princess Ann of Denmark, and also to notify to him that he had been chosen one of the Knights Companions of the Garter, along with the King of France. On the 21st April, 1600, he was appointed Master of the Horse to Queen Elizabeth. The same office was conferred upon him after the accession of King James (15th January, 1604), with the payment of one hundred marks per annum for life, and in the following year he was named one of the Lords Commissioners for exercising the office of Earl-Marshal of England. He resigned the office of Master of the Horse, January 1, 1615, and the following day was constituted Lord Privy Seal, of which high office he had a renewed grant, March 27, 1617, with an annual fee of £1,500 during his life. Three years later he was honoured with the command of his sovereign to sit in the Court of Requests with the masters there, the king, as it is recorded, "deeming it unfit that so great a magistrate should not have a seat of judicature." He married the Lady Elizabeth,* one of the daughters of Francis, second Earl of Huntingdon, by Katharine, his wife, daughter and coheir of Henry Pole, Lord Montagu, and grand-daughter of Margaret, Countess of Salisbury, which Margaret was the daughter and sole heir of George Plantagenet, Duke of Clarence, younger brother of Edward IV. He died at his house in the Strand, March 3, 1627, and was buried at Ragland. William, his eldest son, having pre-deceased him, the honours devolved upon his second son, Henry Somerset, who succeeded as fourth earl, and was advanced to the dignity of Marquis of Worcester, November 2, 1642, his eldest son, Edward, the second marquis, born in 1601, being famed as the inventor of the steam-engine.

* The youngest sister of the Lady Elizabeth was the beautiful Lady Mary Hastings, of whom the following circumstance is related:—"John Vassilivich, Grand Duke and Emperor of Russia, having a desire to marry an English lady, was told of the Lady Mary Hastings, who, being of the blood royal, he began to affect: whereupon, making his desire known to Queen Elizabeth, who did well approve thereof, he sent over Theodore Pessemskoie, a nobleman of great account, his ambassador, who, in the name of his master, offered great advantages to the Queen in the event of the marriage. The Queen hereupon caused the lady to be attended with divers ladies and young noblemen, that so the ambassador might have a sight of her, which was accomplished in York House Garden, near Charing Cross, London. There was the envoy brought into her presence, and casting down his countenance, fell prostrate before her; then rising back, with his face still towards her (the lady, with the rest, admiring at the strange salutation), he said, by his interpreter, 'it sufficed him to behold the angelic presence of her who, he hoped, would be his master's spouse and empress.'" The marriage, however, did not take place, and the lady died unmarried.

THE LORD ADMIRALL, pp. 16, 17.

ARMS.—*Gu.*, a bend between six cross crosslets, fitchée, *arg.*, differenced by a mullet. The shield encircled by a garter with the motto of the order inscribed thereon, and ensigned with an earl's coronet. Excepting the mark of cadency, these arms are identical with those of "The Lord Treasvrer," described on page 115, being "Howard Ancient," and omitting the "Flodden Augmentation" already noticed.

Charles, second Lord Howard of Effingham, Lord High Admiral of England, was the eldest son of William Lord Howard, by his second wife, Margaret, daughter of Sir Thomas Grammage, Knt., and grandson of Thomas, second Duke of Norfolk, by whom the "Flodden Augmentation" above alluded to was obtained. Lord Howard was born in 1536, and in early life assumed the profession of arms. In 1569 he distinguished himself in the suppression of the rebellion headed by the earls of Northumberland and Westmoreland, which had for its object the liberation of the Scottish queen and the re-establishment of the Roman Catholic religion in England. On the death of his father, January 21, 1573, he succeeded to the barony, and on the 24th April in the following year was installed a Knight of the Garter. On the 4th July he was made Lord High Admiral of England, having previously held the office of Lord Chamberlain, and in this capacity he rendered great service to his country; he commanded the fleet fitted out to oppose the Spanish Armada in 1588, and, aided by the winds, succeeded in effecting the total destruction of that powerful armament. In 1596 he was joined with the Earl of Essex in the expedition against Cadiz, and, as a reward for his services in destroying the Spanish fleet there, was on the 23rd October created Earl of Nottingham. In August, 1599, he was named Lieutenant-General of England, and in the following year he suppressed the insurrection raised by Lord Essex, and effected the capture of that rash and presumptuous nobleman. He was present at the death of Queen Elizabeth, and officiated as Lord High Steward of England at the coronation of her successor, James I., during the early part of whose reign he was employed upon several diplomatic missions of importance.

The earl retired from public life in 1618, and died on the 14th December, 1624, at the advanced age of eighty-four, having throughout his long career retained, with unstained honour, the esteem and confidence of his sovereign and his countrymen. Fuller, in his quaint manner, thus speaks of him :—

"An hearty gentleman, and cordial to his sovereign, of a most proper person, one reason why Queen Elizabeth (who, though she did not value a jewel by, valued it the more for, a fair case) reflected so much on him. His service in the 88th is notoriously known, when, at the first news of the Spanish approach, he towed at a cable with his own hands, to draw out the harbour-bound ships into the sea. I dare boldly say he drew more, though not by his person, by his presence and example, than any ten in the place. True it is, he was no deep seaman, (not to be expected from one of his extraction,) but had skill enough to know those who had more skill than himself and to follow their instructions; and would not starve the Queen's service by feeding his own sturdy wilfulness, but was ruled by the experienced in sea matters, the Queen having a navy of *oak* and an admiral of *osier*."

The "Lord Admirall" married, first, Catherine, daughter of Henry Cary, Lord Hunsdon, by whom he had two sons and three daughters; and secondly, Margaret, daughter of James Stewart, Earl of Murray, by whom he had two sons. He was succeeded in the earldom by his second but eldest surviving son, Charles Howard, who died without male issue, in 1642, when the honours devolved upon his half-brother.

THE DVKE OF LENOX, pp. 18, 19.

ARMS.—*Az.*, three fleurs-de-lys, *or* (France Modern), on a bordure, *gu.*, semée de fermaux, *or*. The shield encircled with garter inscribed with the motto of the order and ensigned with a ducal coronet.

ARMS AND PERSONAGES. 121

Lodowick, son of Esme Stuart, Duke of Lenox in the peerage of Scotland, and grandson of John Lord d'Aubignie, younger brother of Matthew Earl of Lenox, the grandfather of King James, bore also the titles of Lord Darnley, Tarbolton, and Methuen, and held the offices of Lord Great Chamberlain, Admiral of Scotland, and Lord Steward of the King's Household. On the accession of James he was sworn of the Privy Council, and bore the sword before that sovereign on his entry into London, May 7, 1603. On the 2nd July in the same year he was installed a Knight of the Garter, and afterwards (October 6, 4th James I.) advanced to the dignity of a baron of the realm by the title of Lord Settrington of Settrington, in the county of York, and on the same day created Earl of Richmond. In 1613, on the marriage of the Princess Elizabeth with Frederick, the Elector Palatine, he was appointed one of the commissioners to accompany the Elector on his return with his bride to the Castle of Heidelberg, and on the 17th May, 21st James I., he was created Earl of Newcastle-upon-Tyne* and Duke of Richmond. He died suddenly at his lodging at Whitehall, Monday, February 16, 1623, as he was preparing to go to Parliament then sitting; and on the 19th April his body was removed with all magnificence from Ely House, in Holborn, to Westminster, and there interred in Henry the Seventh's Chapel, in which a stately tomb has been erected to his memory. The Duke of Lenox married (first), Sophia, daughter of William Earl of Ruthven, and sister to the Earl of Gowrie; (secondly), —— sister of Sir Hugh Campbell and widow of Robert Montgomerie of Eglintoun; and (thirdly), Frances, daughter of Thomas Howard, Viscount Bindon, and widow of Edward Earl of Hertford, but left no issue by any; whereupon his younger brother, Esme Stuart, Lord D'Aubigne, Baron Clifton, of Leighton-Bromswold, in Lincolnshire, and Earl of March, became heir.

---

* Beatson, in his *Political Index*, says he was created Earl of Newcastle-on-Tyne 2nd James, 1604.

THE MARQVESSE OF BVCKINGHAM, pp. 20, 21.

ARMS.—*Arg.*, on a cross, *gu.*, five escallops *or*, a martlet of the second.

George Villiers, Marquess of Buckingham, the unworthy favourite of James and his son Charles I., was the eldest son by the second marriage of Sir George Villiers, Knight, the representative of an ancient family in Leicestershire, and was born August 28, 1592. He completed his education in France, and returning to England from his travels when about twenty-one, was introduced to the court of King James, where his natural accomplishments, his easy and graceful demeanour, and attractive presence, soon gained for him the favour of the king, over whom he eventually acquired entire dominion. In the first week of January, 1616, he was appointed Master of the Horse; on the 7th July in the same year he was installed a Knight of the Garter; and on Tuesday, the 27th August following, was created Viscount Villiers and Baron of Whaddon. On Sunday, the 5th January, in the succeeding year, he was elevated to the Earldom of Buckingham, on the 4th February he was sworn a Privy Councillor, and on New Year's day in the following year advanced to the dignity of Marquess of Buckingham. On the 18th May, 1623, the King created him Earl of Coventry and Duke of Buckingham, and he was afterwards made Chancellor of the University of Cambridge. He rapidly rose to the highest offices of the state, was made Chief Justice in Eyre, Warden of the Cinque Ports, Master of the King's Bench, Steward of Westminster, Constable of Windsor, and Lord High Admiral of England. The history of the court at this period is simply that of Buckingham: he became the dispenser of all favours and honours, and conducted himself with so much pride and arrogance as to excite popular hatred and disgust. He introduced all his kindred to the court, had them quartered at Whitehall, and made their fortunes by places, pensions, and marriages. In 1623 he accompanied Prince Charles on his romantic mission to Spain; but receiving some slight from the court at Madrid, he resolved to break off the match with the Infanta, which resulted eventually in a war with Spain. After the death of James, Buckingham continued the favourite minister of Charles I., who surrendered himself to his pernicious counsels. In 1627, through his instigation, war was declared against France, and in June of that year a fleet was sent out, of which he took the command; but his measures were so ill-concerted, that he lost two-thirds of his forces. He had now entirely lost the confidence of the Commons, who prayed the king to dismiss him, declaring that his inglorious expedition had tarnished the honour of the nation, annihilated its commerce, and greatly diminished its navy. He returned to Portsmouth to refit his shattered armament, but before he could again set sail, he was assassinated by John Felton, an Irishman of good family, who had served under him as lieutenant, and instantly expired, August 23, 1638, to the great grief of the king, who mourned the loss of his favourite, and the scarcely concealed satisfaction of the nation, which rejoiced at the deliverance it had experienced.

By his wife Catharine, daughter of Francis, sixth Earl of Rutland, who, surviving him, afterwards married Randolph Macdonald, Earl and Marquess of Antrim, he had four children: Charles, who died an infant; George, the witty duke, who succeeded him; Francis, who fell in the civil wars; and Mary, afterwards Duchess of Richmond.

THE LORD CHAMBERLINE, pp. 22, 23.

ARMS.—Per pale *az.* and *gu.*, three lions rampant, two and one, *arg.;* the shield encircled with a garter, inscribed with the motto of the order, and ensigned with the coronet of an earl.

William Herbert, third Earl of Pembroke, was the eldest son of Henry Herbert, the second earl, by his third wife, Mary,* daughter of Sir Henry Sidney, of Penshurst, in Kent, and sister of Sir Philip Sidney, styled the "Incomparable," whose "learning, beauty, chivalry, and grace shed a lustre on the most glorious reign recorded in the English annals." William Herbert was born at Wilton House, the family seat, April 8, 1580, and received his education at New College, Oxford. On the 2nd July, 1603, he was installed a Knight of the Garter; in 1615 he was appointed to succeed Robert Carr, Earl of Somerset, who had been convicted of the murder of Sir Thomas Overbury, in the office of Lord Chamberlain of the Household; and on the 23rd December of the same year he was sworn a Privy Councillor. He took a prominent part in public affairs; and when, on the occasion of Buckingham's impeachment in the Parliament of Charles I., Sir John Eliot and Sir Dudley Digges were committed to the Tower, he headed

---

* The Lady Mary Sidney was celebrated for her beauty, intelligence, and goodness. She was the author of several religious works and poetical pieces, and translated from the French the *Discourse of Life and Death*, by Philippe de Mornay. To her, "a principal ornament to the family of the Sidneis," Sir Philip Sidney dedicated the celebrated romance of "Arcadia," which he wrote for her pleasure. She lived to an advanced age, and died, after a widowhood of twenty years, at her house in Aldersgate Street, London, September 25, 1621. To her memory Ben Jonson wrote the inscription in the cathedral of Salisbury so much admired:—

> " Underneath this marble hearse
> Lies the subject of all verse—
> Sidney's sister, Pembroke's mother.
> Death ! ere thou hast slain another,
> Fair and wise and good as she,
> Time shall throw a dart at thee."

ARMS AND PERSONAGES.

the opposition in the House of Lords, at the time holding four proxies, and in the previous Parliament ten, an accumulation of suffrages in one person that led to an order of the House, which is now its established regulation, that no peer can hold more than two proxies.* He died April 10, 1630, and was succeeded by his brother Philip Herbert, Earl of Montgomery, having no surviving issue by his countess Mary, eldest daughter of Gilbert Earl of Shrewsbury.

The Earl of Pembroke was not less distinguished as a writer than as a statesman; he was an accomplished poet and a great patron of learning. To him and his brother "Philip, Earle of Mountgomerie," "the moste honorable and woerthie brothers," "patrons of learning and cheualrie," Otho van Veen, in 1608, dedicated his *Armorum Emblemata*.

In 1626 he was elected Chancellor of the University of Oxford, of which, in his lifetime, he was a liberal benefactor, and to which, at his death, he bequeathed a valuable collection of manuscripts.

THE EARLE OF ARVNDELL, pp. 24, 25.

ARMS.—Howard Ancient: *gu.*, a bend between six crosses crosslet, fitchée, *arg.*; the shield encircled with a garter bearing the motto of the order, and ensigned with an earl's coronet.

Thomas Howard, Earl of Arundel, the only son of Philip Earl of Arundel, by Ann, daughter of Thomas, and sister and coheir to George, Lord Dacre of Gillesland, was born July 17, 1592. Earl Philip, a zealous Roman Catholic, having been attainted, was committed to the Tower, and died a prisoner there in 1595, his son being deprived by the attainder of the honours and the greater part of the estates of the family, though styled by courtesy, during

* Lords' Journals, p. 507.

the remaining part of Elizabeth's reign, Lord Maltravers. The accession of King James opened fairer prospects to the Howard family, and in the first year of that king's reign he was restored by Act of Parliament to the title of Earl of Arundel, and to all honours dependent upon it, though not to all the possessions; and also to the honour, dignity, and state of Earl of Surrey, and to such dignity and baronies as Thomas Duke of Norfolk, his grandfather, forfeited through his attachment to the ill-fated mother of James, Mary Queen of Scots. His health failing, he resolved to travel, and in 1609 passed through France into Italy, returning in 1611 on the 13th May, in which year he was installed a Knight of the Garter. In 1613 he was appointed one of the embassy to accompany the Princess Elizabeth, married to the Elector Palatine, into Germany. Thence he travelled again into Italy, where he cultivated a taste for architecture, sculpture, and antiquities, and returned to England in November, 1614; after which he was sworn of the Privy Council, named one of the six commissioners of the office of Earl-Marshal, and in 1621 appointed hereditary Earl-Marshal of England, an office that is still held by his descendants, the Dukes of Norfolk. Having about this time given offence to Lord Spencer in the House of Lords,* and refusing to give satisfaction when so enjoined, he was committed to the Tower, and there kept a prisoner until willing to make submission. Shortly after the accession of Charles I. he was again committed to the Tower, the reason assigned being that his heir, the Lord Maltravers, had married the Lady Elizabeth Stuart, eldest daughter of Esme, Duke of Lenox, without the king's knowledge and consent. His release was effected through the instrumentality of Dr. Williams, Bishop of Lincoln, and he was shortly afterwards again admitted to court, where

* The Lord Spencer of Wormleighton, in addressing the House, having made allusion to some act committed by their great ancestors, which gave umbrage to the earl, he said, "My lord, when these things you speak of were doing, your ancestors were keeping sheep"; to which Lord Spencer rejoined: "When my ancestors, as you say, were keeping sheep, your ancestors were plotting treason."

he so far recovered the king's favour, that in 1631 he was sent on a mission into Holland to condole with the Queen of Bohemia on the death of her husband, and at the same time appointed Ambassador to the States-General. In 1633 he was ordered to attend the king in his journey to Scotland, and three years later was sent on a diplomatic mission to the emperor Ferdinand III. In 1638 he was appointed general of the army raised against the Scots; afterwards he was made Lord Steward of the King's Household, and in 1640, upon the advance of the Scots into England, was named General of the South of the Trent. Upon the trial of the Earl of Strafford in 1641, he sat as Lord High Steward of England. Shortly afterwards he resigned the office of Lord Steward of the King's Household, and in September, 1641, he accompanied the queen-mother, who was constrained to leave the country in consequence of the unhappy difficulties arising between Charles and his Parliament, but he returned shortly afterwards. In February of the following year he left England for the last time, attending the Princess of Orange into Holland. Thence he visited Antwerp, afterwards he journeyed into France, and finally passed into Italy, where he spent the remainder of his life. He died at Padua, September 14, 1646, having some two years before, June 6, 1644, been elevated to the Earldom of Norfolk.

The Earl is described as of a stately presence and a great master of order and ceremony, more learned in men and manners than in books, yet understanding the Latin tongue, as well as being master of the Italian. Walker says, " he was in religion no bigot nor puritan ; and professed most to affect moral virtues than nice questions and controversies."* He was a great patron of the arts, especially of sculpture and painting, and spent large sums in the collection of such works, employing many persons in Italy, Greece, and other parts of Europe where curiosities could be obtained. At his death the unrivalled collection

---

* Sir Edward Walker's " *Historical Discourses,*" ed. 1705.

of antiquities he had formed was divided, and in 1688, Henry, sixth Duke of Norfolk, presented the University of Oxford with a considerable portion of his moiety, including the celebrated Parian Chronicle, which, with other ancient inscribed stones accompanying it, are termed the *Arundelian Marbles*.

Lord Arundel married, in 1606, the Lady Athelia Talbot, third daughter, and eventually sole heir, of Gilbert Earl of Shrewsbury, and was succeeded in the honours by his second son, Henry Frederick, his eldest son, James Lord Mowbray and Maltravers, having predeceased him.

THE EARLE OF SOVTH-HAMPTON, pp. 26, 27.

ARMS.—*Az.*, a cross *or*. between four hawks, closed, *arg.*,* encircled with a garter bearing the motto of the order, and ensigned with the coronet of an earl.

Henry Wriothesley, third Earl of Southampton, only son of Henry, the second earl, by Mary, daughter of Anthony Viscount Montagu, and grandson of Thomas Wriothesley, Lord Chancellor of England in the time of Henry VIII., was born in 1573, and succeeded to the title on the death of his father, 23 Elizabeth (1580-81). In 1596 he accompanied his friend, the Earl of Essex, in the expedition against Spain, and contributed to the capture of Cadiz. Afterwards he returned to Ireland, and joining in the insurrection headed by Essex, he was arraigned at Westminster, and with the earl, February 19, 1600, found guilty, and committed to the Tower, where he remained a close prisoner until the accession of James I., when he obtained his release. On the 2nd July, 1603, he was installed a Knight of the Garter, and on the 21st of the same month received a new patent for the title and dignity of Earl of Southampton, with like rights and pri-

---

* This coat is almost identical with that of the College of Arms or Heralds' College, London, derived from Wriothesley, one of the early Garters.

vileges as he formerly enjoyed. In 1613 the earl entertained King James; in March, 1616, he was one of the noblemen appointed to attend the king with the queen and Prince Charles in their journey from Whitehall to Edinburgh; and on Friday, the 30th April, 1613, he was sworn of the Privy Council. In 1624 he accompanied the expedition to Holland to assist the Prince Maurice of Orange, and died at Bergen-op-zoom in November of the same year, having had issue by his wife Elizabeth, daughter of John Vernon, of Hodnet, in the county of Salop, John, who died in the Netherlands in the lifetime of his father; Thomas, who succeeded; and three daughters,—Penelope, married to William Lord Spencer, of Wormleighton; Ann, married to Robert Wallop, of Farley, Esq.; and Elizabeth, married to Sir Thomas Estcourt, Knt., a Master in Chancery.

The Earl of Southampton was scarcely less distinguished as a patron of letters than for his political talent. He is now chiefly remembered as the friend of Shakespeare, who dedicated to him "the first heir of his invention," the *Venus and Adonis*, and *The Rape of Lucrece*.

THE EARLE OF HERTFORD, pp. 28, 29.

ARMS.—*Or*, on a pile, *gu.*, between six fleurs-de-lys, *az.*, three lions of England being the coat of augmentation granted by King Henry VIII. on his marriage with Lady Jane Seymour; the shield ensigned with an earl's coronet.

Edward Seymour, by whom these arms were borne, was the eldest son, by the second marriage, of Edward Seymour, Duke of Somerset, who as Protector grasped the sceptre of unlimited authority, and swayed it with all the attributes of royalty during the two years of the minority of King Edward VI. His mother was Ann, daughter of Sir Edward Stanhope, of Sudbury, in the county of Suffolk,

Knt., by Elizabeth his wife, great-granddaughter of William Bouchier, Earl of Ewe, in Normandy, by Ann his wife, daughter and eventually sole heir of Thomas of Woodstock, Duke of Gloucester, youngest son of Edward III. The *Protector* Somerset having been charged with treasonable designs against the lives of some of the Privy Councillors, was brought to the block January 22, 1552. Being attainted, the titles which, according to the special limitation of the patents of creation, devolved upon the issue by his second marriage, of course became forfeited, together with lands of great annual value. Thus deprived of all his titles and of the great part of his inheritance, the youthful Edward Seymour continued in a disconsolate condition until the first year of Queen Elizabeth, when, before her coronation, that sovereign created him Baron Beauchamp of Hacche and Earl of Hertford; and, doubtless, he would have been restored to the dukedom of Somerset, had he not incurred the queen's displeasure by marrying the Lady Catharine Grey, daughter and heir of Henry Duke of Suffolk, the sister of the amiable and unfortunate Lady Jane Grey, and the granddaughter maternally of Charles Brandon, Duke of Suffolk, by Mary, Queen Dowager of France, sister of King Henry VIII. Upon the discovery of her pregnancy in 1563, both were committed to the Tower, where the countess died a prisoner in 1567, after giving birth to two sons,—Edward, who died in childhood, and Edward Lord Beauchamp, who in the 6th James I., 1608-9, obtained letters patent for the enjoyment of the title of Earl of Hertford. The earl was detained a prisoner in the Tower for nine years, and fined by the Star Chamber £15,000 for having vitiated a maid of the royal blood. The validity of his marriage with the Lady Catharine Grey was afterwards tried and established at common law. After his enlargement, the earl only once acted in a public capacity, the occasion being in 1605, when, on the 19th April, he was sent as ambassador to the Archduke of Austria, to ratify and conclude a peace, the preliminaries of which had been previously settled, and in which mission he was accompanied by two barons, sixteen knights, and many gentlemen of quality, his retinue numbering three hundred persons, most of them being his own servants, in very rich liveries. The earl, who lived to an advanced age, died in 1621, and was succeeded by his grandson, Sir William Seymour, second son of Edward Lord Beauchamp.

THE EARLE OF ESSEX, pp. 30, 31.

ARMS.—*Arg.*, a fesse, *gu.*, in chief three torteaux, the shield ensigned with an earl's coronet.

Robert, third Earl of Essex, was the only son of Robert Devereux, second earl, the distinguished but unfortunate favourite of Queen Elizabeth, by Frances, daughter and heir of Sir Francis Walsingham, Elizabeth's Secretary of State, and the widow of the gallant, the amiable, and accomplished Sir Philip Sidney. He was born in 1592, entered at Merton College, Oxford, in his tenth year, and restored to the family honours by James I. in 1603, two years after his father's decapitation. In 1620 he served under Sir Horace Vere in the expedition sent to the assistance of Frederick, the Elector Palatine; afterwards he was with Prince Maurice in Holland, and subsequently held several military commands. As already stated (p. 91), he was named among "the Illustrious & Heroyicall Princes," to whose "Eternall Memorie" the twenty-four leaves of *Honour in its Perfection* were, in 1624, dedicated. In May, 1638, he was installed a Knight of the Garter, and remained attached to the royal cause until the breaking out of the civil war, when he joined the popular party, and in July, 1642, accepted a general's commission, and a command in the Parliamentary army. He defeated the king's forces at Edge Hill, the first place in which the two armies were put in array against each other, October 23, 1642; subsequently he took Reading, raised the siege of Gloucester, and fought in the first battle of Newbury, but in 1645 was deprived of his command by the "self-denying ordinance," under which all members of Parliament were excluded from civil and military employment. He died at Essex House, in the Strand, a mansion bequeathed to his father by Dudley Earl of Leicester, September 14, 1646, and was buried with national obsequies in Westminster Abbey, the two Houses of Parliament attending his funeral.

At the age of fourteen the earl was betrothed to the Lady Frances, daughter of Thomas Howard, Earl of Suffolk; but from this lady, who afterwards became notorious as the wife of Robert Carr, Earl of Somerset, he obtained a divorce, and married, secondly, Elizabeth, daughter of Sir William Powlett, of Eddington, in Wiltshire, by whom he had an only son, who died in infancy; and hence the earldom of Ewe and Essex expired, the barony of Ferrers fell into abeyance, and the viscounty of Hereford devolved upon his kinsman Sir Walter Devereux.

THE EARLE OF DORSET, pp. 32, 33.

ARMS.—Quarterly *or*, and *gu.*; over all, a bend, *vair.*; the shield ensigned with the coronet of an earl.

This representative of the ancient and very distinguished family of Sackville, Richard, third Earl of Dorset, was the second son (his elder brother, Thomas, having died unmarried in 1586) of Robert, the second earl, by Margaret, daughter of Thomas Duke of Norfolk, beheaded in 1572, and the grandson of Thomas Sackville, the famous Lord Buckhurst, and first Earl of Dorset,* who succeeded Burleigh as Lord Treasurer of England, and died whilst sitting at

---

* Thomas, the first earl, was no less famous as a man of letters than as a statesman. He is celebrated as the author of the earliest English tragedy in blank verse, *Gorboduc*, which has been praised by Sidney for its "notable moralitie," and is believed to have given rise to the *Fairy Queen*; he also wrote *The Induction to a Mirrour for Magistrates*, one of the noblest poems in the language, and *The Complaint of Henry Duke of Buckingham*, &c.

the council-table, April 19, 1608, at the age of eighty-two. Richard Sackville, who was born in 1589, succeeded to the earldom on the death of his father, who had enjoyed the family honours only a few months, February 23, 1609, being then twenty years of age; and two days afterwards, February 25th, married the Lady Ann Clifford,* sole daughter and heir to George Earl of Cumberland, and nearly related to the royal family of England by the marriage of her grandfather with the niece of Henry VIII. He rebuilt the chapel at Withiham, the burial-place of his progenitors; but, having wasted a large portion of his patrimony, he eventually parted with the stately mansion of Knole,† which his grandfather, the Lord Treasurer, had had bestowed upon him by his royal mistress. He died at Dorset House, Fleet-street, London, on the 28th March, 1624, in the thirty-fifth year of his age, and was buried at Withiham, having had issue Thomas, who died in infancy, and two daughters,—Margaret, married to John Earl of Thanet, and Isabella, married to James Earl of Northampton. Having no surviving male issue, he was succeeded in the title by his younger brother, Sir Edward Sackville.

* This celebrated lady, who married as her second husband Philip Herbert, Earl of Pembroke and Montgomery, possessed considerable literary ability, but was chiefly distinguished by her high spirit, and a career of munificence, hospitality, and usefulness, that has thrown much veneration round her memory. She restored the castles of Skipton, Brougham, Appleby, and Pendragon, and was as diligent in repairing the churches as the fortified mansions of her ancestors. After the death of her mother, whose memory she greatly revered, she caused a pillar, bearing a suitable inscription, to be erected on the road between Appleby and Penrith, the spot where they had held their last interview :—

"That modest stone which pious Pembroke rear'd,
Which still records beyond the pencil's power
The silent sorrow of a parting hour."—*Pleasures of Memory.*

Her high spirit was characteristically displayed in the reply she gave to Williamson, Secretary of State to Charles II., who wished to nominate a member of Parliament for her borough of Appleby:—"I have been bullied by a usurper, I have been neglected by a court, but I will not be dictated to by a subject : your man sha'n't stand." She died on the 22nd March, 1676, in the eighty-eighth year of her age, and was buried, by her express desire, by the side of her mother in the church of Appleby.

† The mansion, with the demesne of Knole, was repurchased by Richard, the fifth Earl of Dorset, and it has ever since continued in this illustrious family.

THE EARLE OF MOVNTGOMERY, pp. 34, 35.

ARMS.—Per pale, *az.* and *gu.*, three lions, rampant, *arg.*, differenced by a crescent, the mark of cadency of a second son; the shield encircled by a garter inscribed with the motto of the order, and ensigned with an earl's coronet.

Philip Herbert, Earl of Montgomery, the "memorable simpleton," as Walpole styles him, who dimmed the lustre of an honoured name by his cowardice, arrogance, and folly, was the younger brother of William, third Earl of Pembroke, to whom, as Lord Chamberlain, reference has already been made, and second son of Henry, the second earl, by Mary, second daughter of Sir Henry Sidney, Knt. On the 4th May, 1605, he was created by James I. Baron Herbert of Shurland, in the Isle of Sheppy, and Earl of Montgomery, and on the 20th May, 1608, was installed a Knight of the Garter, being at the same time one of the gentlemen of the chamber to the king. He held the office of Lord Chamberlain of the Household to Charles I., and became Chancellor of the University of Oxford, though he was so illiterate that he could scarcely write his own name.* On the death of his elder brother without surviving issue, April 10, 1630, he succeeded to the earldom of Pembroke, which had been conferred on his grandfather, William Herbert, who married Ann, sister to Queen Katherine Parr, the last wife of Henry VIII. During his lifetime, Charles I. was a frequent visitor at Wilton House, the stately residence of the Pembroke family. Aubrey says the king "did love Wilton above all places, and came there every summer. It was he that did put Philip, first [fourth?] Earle of Pembroke, upon making the magnificent garden and grotto, and to build that side of the house that fronts the garden, with two stately pavilions at each end." He is described as a nobleman profligate in his private habits and unprincipled

---

* *Athenæ Oxon.*, vol. i. p. 546.

in public life, but withal a patron of learning; as already stated, he was one of the two "moste honorable and woerthie brothers," "patrons of learning and cheualrie," to whom Otho van Veen dedicated his *Amorvm Emblemata;* and to him and his brother, Earl William, "the most noble and incomparable pair of brothers," Heminge and Condell inscribed the first folio edition of Shakspeare's plays. His death occurred January 23, 1650.

The Earl of Montgomery was twice married; first, in 1604,* to Susan, youngest daughter and eventually coheir to Edward Vere, Earl of Oxford, the courtier poet of Elizabeth's time, by whom he had issue Charles, who married in 1634 the Lady Mary Villiers, only daughter of George Duke of Buckingham, but died in a few weeks afterwards without cohabitation; Philip, who succeeded as fifth Earl of Pembroke; William and John, who both died issueless; James, married to Jane, daughter of Sir Robert Spiller, Knt., of Laleham, in Middlesex; and a daughter, Ann-Sophia, married to Robert Dormer, Earl of Carnarvon. He married, secondly, the celebrated Lady Ann Clifford, Duchess Dowager of Dorset, of whom mention has already been made—an union that caused that lady much sorrow and anxiety—but by her had no issue.

* The marriage was celebrated with great pomp at Whitehall, the king giving away the bride. Sir Dudley Carleton, in a letter to Mr. Winwood, gives a description of the entertainment, which is interesting as illustrating the manners of the times :—"There was," he says, "no small loss that night of chains and jewels, and many great ladies were made shorter by the skirts, and were very well served that they could keep cut no better. The presents of plate and other things given by the noblemen were valued at £2,500; but that which made it a good marriage was a gift of the king's, of £500 land for the bride's jointure. They were lodged in the Council Chamber, where the king, in his shirt and nightgown, gave them a *réveille-matin* before they were up, and spent a good time in or upon the bed : chuse which you will believe. No ceremony was omitted of bridecakes, points, garters, and gloves, which have been ever since the livery of the court; and at night there was sewing into the sheet, casting off the bride's left hose, and many other pretty sorceries."—*Win. Mem.*, vol. ii. p. 43.

THE LORD VISCOVNT LISLE, pp. 36, 37.

ARMS.—*Or*, a pheon, *az*. The shield encircled by a garter inscribed with the motto of the order and ensigned with the coronet of a viscount.

Sir Robert Sidney, Baron Sidney of Penshurst, and Viscount L'Isle, the representative of a family which contributed in no small degree to make the reign of Elizabeth the glory of all time, was the second son of Sir Henry Sidney, of Penshurst, a learned and accomplished knight, in whose arms the youthful King Edward VI. expired, by Mary, daughter of "the great and miserable" John Dudley, Duke of Northumberland, sister to Robert Dudley, Earl of Leicester, and the younger brother of Sir Philip Sidney, the eloquent poet, the able statesman and noble soldier, the "darling of his time," the "chiefest jewel of a crown," the "diamond of the court of Queen Elizabeth." Sir Robert Sidney served under his uncle, the Earl of Leicester, in the Netherlands, and in 1597-8, being joined by Sir Frances Vere in the command of the English auxiliaries sent against the Spaniards, he shared in the honour of the victory gained at Turnhoult, in Brabant. He held the office of Lord Chamberlain to Queen Elizabeth, and on the accession of King James, was constituted Governor of Flushing. On the 13th May, in the first year of that king's reign, he was made a baron of the realm by the title of Lord Sidney of Penshurst, in the county of Kent, and on the 4th May, 1605, was created Viscount L'Isle. In April, 1613, he was named one of the principal commissioners to accompany the Princess Elizabeth, then lately married, and her husband, Frederick, the Elector Palatine, to Germany; on the 7th July, 1616, he was installed a Knight of the Garter, and on the 2nd August, 1618, was advanced to the dignity of Earl of Leicester. He died July 13, 1626, and was buried at Penshurst, having been twice married; first to Barbara, daughter and heir of John Gammage, Esq., by whom he had three sons,—Sir William, who died unmarried; Henry, who died young; and Robert, his heir;—and secondly, to the widow of Sir Thomas Smith, Knight.

His youngest and only surviving son, Robert Sidney, who succeeded as second Earl of Leicester, was the father of Algernon Sidney, whose name is scarcely less renowned in history than that of his great uncle Sir Philip, and who, through the iniquitous Jeffreys, was implicated in the Rye-House Plot, and illegally put to death in 1683.

THE LORD VISCOVNT WALLINGFORD,
pp. 38, 39.

ARMS.—*Az.*, a cross recercele voided, semée of cross crosslets, *or;* the shield encircled by a garter inscribed with the motto of the order, and ensigned with the coronet of a viscount.

Sir William Knollys, Viscount Wallingford, the "noble personage" to whom these arms belonged, was the second but eldest surviving son of Sir Francis Knollys, K.G., an eminent lawyer of Elizabeth's reign, descended from the renowned Sir Robert Knollys, K.G., the gallant companion in arms of Edward the Black Prince, his mother being Catharine, daughter of William Cary, Esquire, by Mary, sister of the unfortunate Queen Ann Boleyn. He was born in 1544, and shortly after the accession of King James (Friday, May 20, 1603), was created a baron of the realm by the title of Lord Knollys of Grays.

In the twelfth year of that king's reign he was made Master of the Court of Wards, and subsequently installed a Knight of the Garter; on the 7th November, 1616, he was raised to the dignity of a viscount by the title of Viscount Wallingford, and on the 14th of the same month he was named Lord Treasurer of the King's Household. After the death of James, Lord Wallingford continued in favour at court, and on the 18th August, 2 Charles I. (1626), was elevated to the earldom of Banbury, with precedence of all earls created before him. He died on the 25th May, 1632, in the 88th year of his age, and was buried at the church of Grays, in Oxfordshire.

The earl married, first, Dorothy, widow of Edmund Lord Chandos, and sister of John Lord Bray, who bore him no issue; and, secondly, January 19, 1605, Elizabeth, eldest daughter of Thomas, first Earl of Suffolk, who surviving him, became the wife of Edward, fourth Lord Vaux of Harrowden. This lady had two sons born during the lifetime of the earl; viz., Edward, born 1627, aged five years, one month, and fifteen days, at the earl's decease, who was slain in a quarrel in France, leaving no issue; and Nicholas, born January, 1630, who died 14th March, 1673-4, having sat as Earl of Banbury in the Convention Parliament; though his claim to the family honours was disputed on the ground of illegitimacy, the belief being that he was a son of Lord Vaux, whom his mother afterwards married, rather than of the Earl of Banbury, who must have been eighty-four years of age at the time of his birth.

THE BISHOP OF LONDON, pp. 40, 41.

ARMS.—*Gu.*, two swords, in saltire, *arg.*, pommels *or ;* the arms of the see of London, ensigned with a mitre.

John King, Bishop of London, an eminent preacher at court in the reigns of Elizabeth and James I., was born at Wornal, in Buckinghamshire, 1559. He received his education at Westminster, and after completing his academical career at Christ Church, Oxford, was appointed chaplain to Queen Elizabeth. In 1590 he was named Archdeacon of Nottingham, and in 1605 preferred to the deanery of Christ Church, and made Vice-Chancellor of the University of Oxford. Afterwards he was removed

ARMS AND PERSONAGES.   139

to the see of London, and consecrated bishop on Sunday, September 11, 1611. He is said to have been a great master of his tongue and his pen. King James styled him "the king of preachers," and Lord Chief Justice Coke declared that "he was the best speaker in the Star Chamber of his time." He died March 30, 1621, and was buried under a plain stone in St. Paul's, on which was inscribed only the word "*Resurgam.*" It has been alleged that he died in the communion of the Church of Rome, but the calumny has been amply refuted.

Bishop King had a son Henry, born at Wornal, 1591, who became chaplain to James I., and in 1641 was consecrated Bishop of Chichester. Like his father, he was a celebrated preacher, and wrote a metrical version of the Book of Psalms, and was the author of several poems, sermons, and letters. Another son of the Bishop of London was John King, born in 1596, who was successively Orator of Oxford University, Prebendary of St. Paul's, and Canon of Windsor.

THE BISHOP OF WINCHESTER, pp. 42, 43.

ARMS.—*Gu.*, two keys, addorsed, in bend, the uppermost *arg.*, the other *or*, a sword interposed between them, in bend sinister, of the second, hilt and pommel gold; the arms of the see of Winchester impaling, *arg.*, three lozenges conjoined, in fesse, *gu.*, within a bordure, *sa.*, differenced by an annulet, for Montagu; the shield ensigned with a bishop's mitre.

James Montagu, Bishop of Winchester, who bore the armorial insignia above described, was one of the six sons of Sir Edward Montagu, Knt., by Elizabeth, daughter of Sir James Harington, of Exton, in Rutlandshire, and grandson of Sir Edward Montagu, the distinguished lawyer, and Lord Chief Justice of the King's Bench in Henry VIII.'s reign,—the common ancestor of the ducal house of Manchester, of the dukes of Montagu and the earls of Halifax, now extinct. The prelate was born in 1538, and received his education at Christ's Church College, Cambridge, and afterwards became Master of Sydney College, in the same University. On the accession of King James he was named Dean of the Chapel Royal, an appointment that had been vacant during the last eight years of Elizabeth's reign. On the 17th April, 1607, he was consecrated Bishop of Bath and Wells; in October, 1616, he was translated to Winchester, and on Michaelmas-day, 1617, sworn a Privy Councillor at Hampton Court. Dr. Montagu presided over the see of Winchester only for a short period, his death occurring July 20, 1618, in the eightieth year of his age. His remains were conveyed to Bath and there interred in the abbey church, which during his episcopate had been restored at his own expense.

THE BISHOP OF ELY, pp. 44, 45.

ARMS.—*Gu.*, three ducal crowns, two and one, *or;* the arms of the see of Ely, ensigned with a bishop's mitre.

Launcelot Andrews, who presided over the see of Ely at the time the *Mirrour of Maiestie* appeared, was born in the city of London in 1555. From his youth he was remarkable for diligence in his studies and sobriety in his demeanour. He began his academical career at Pembroke Hall, Cambridge, was elected fellow in 1576, and master in 1589. He entered upon the ministry in 1580, and soon became one of the most distinguished preachers of the age. St. Giles's and St. Paul's were long the scene of his labours during the reign of Elizabeth, who made him one of her chaplains, and in 1597 appointed him Prebendary, and in 1601 Dean of Windsor. Dr. Andrews continued in high favour with James I., who admired him beyond all other divines, and in 1605 nominated him Bishop of Ely and Lord Almoner. In 1609 he was translated to the see of Ely; on Michaelmas-day, 1616, he was sworn of the Privy Council;

and on the death of Bishop Montagu was translated to the see of Winchester, the *congé d'élire* to the dean and chapter bearing date December 3, 1618.

In learning Andrews ranked next to Usher; his linguistic acquirements were vast, including Hebrew, Chaldee, Syriac, and Arabic, in addition to five modern languages. "The world," said Fuller, "wanted learning to know how learned this man was." He was included in the commission appointed to translate the Bible, and with nine others was assigned the Pentateuch and historical books, commencing with Joshua and ending with Kings; he also wrote a *Manual of Private Devotions* and other works, and was employed by King James to answer Cardinal Bellarmine's attack upon that monarch's *Defence of the Rights of Kings*. Andrews belonged to what is known as the High Church party, his views being much in accordance with those of Laud, who called him "the light of the Christian world." In Elizabeth's reign he caused scandal by preaching at court "that contrition, without confession and absolution and deeds worthy of repentance, was not sufficient; that the ministers had the two keys of power and knowledge delivered unto them; that whose sins soever they remitted upon earth should be remitted in heaven."[*] His learning was extolled by some of the greatest European scholars, his oratory was irresistibly fascinating, and his moral character was worthy of his fame and office. Of his personal piety no second opinion can be entertained: through life he exercised the charity and hospitality of a Christian bishop, and at his death, which occurred in 1626, he left all his means for the promotion of works of piety and benevolence.

[*] Sidney Letters, vol. ii. 192.

THE LORD ZOVCH, pp. 46, 47.

ARMS.—*Gu.*, ten bezants, *or*, a canton, *ermine.**

Edward, son and heir of George, tenth Lord Zouch of Haryngworth, by Margaret, daughter and coheir of William Welby, of Molton, in Lincolnshire, succeeded as eleventh lord on the death of his father in 1569, being then in his minority. He was a "personage" of considerable note in the reign of Elizabeth, and not less so in that of her successor, James I. In 1587 he was one of the peers who sat in judgment upon the ill-fated Queen of Scots, and was afterwards sent on a diplomatic mission to Scotland to palliate the act. On the 10th June, 1598, he was dispatched to Copenhagen to present the congratulations of the Queen of England to Christian IV., King of Denmark, on the occasion of his marriage with the daughter of the Marquess of Brandenbourg, and in 1601-2 was appointed Lord President of Wales. On the accession of King James, he was continued in his office of Lord President, and on the 11th May, 1603, along with Lord Burghley, was sworn a Privy Councillor at the Charter house, and shortly afterwards was constituted Constable of Dover Castle and Warden of the Cinque Ports for life, during which time Sir Edward Nicholas, afterwards so celebrated, was his secretary. Lord Zouch was the friend of Sir Henry Wotton, the famous diplomatist and political writer, and is said to have been intimately acquainted with Ben Jonson, the dramatist, concerning whom the following circumstance is related in Bridges' *History of Northamptonshire* :—" That eastward from the church of Haryngworth, and contiguous to the old manor-house, are large ruins of the outward walls of a chapel, and against the south wall are the remains of the monument of George Lord Zouch, who died in 1569. At the bottom of the north wall is a small hole communicating with the cellar of the house, which, according to tradition,

* In the *Mirrour* eleven bezants are depicted.

gave occasion to the following lines of the facetious Ben Jonson:—

> 'Whenever I die, let this be my fate,
> To lye by my good lord Zouche;
> That when I am dry, to the tap I may hye,
> And so back again to my couch.'"

Lord Zouch married Eleanor, daughter of Sir John Zouch, of Codnor, and, surviving her, had for his second wife Sarah, daughter of Sir James Harington, of Exton, the sister of Elizabeth, wife of Sir Edward Montagu, and widow, first, of Francis Lord Hastings, and, secondly, of Sir George Kingsmill. His lordship died in 1625, leaving two daughters his coheirs; viz., Elizabeth, married to William Tate, of De la Pre, in Northamptonshire, and Mary, wife of Thomas Leighton, Esq.; but, having no surviving male issue, the barony fell into abeyance, and so remained until 1807, when Sir Cecil Bisshopp preferred a claim to the ancient dignity in right of his mother, descended from Elizabeth, the eldest of the two coheirs of Lord Zouch, and having made good his descent, had summons to Parliament.

THE LORD WINDSOR, pp. 48, 49.

ARMS.—*Gu.*, a saltire, *arg.*, between sixteen cross-crosslets, *or.**

Thomas, sixth Lord Windsor, the last of that surname who enjoyed the title, was the son of Henry, the fifth lord, a nobleman of great qualifications and virtues, by Ann, daughter and coheir of Sir Thomas Revet, of Chippenham, in Kent, Knt. On the death of his father, in 1605, Lord Thomas succeeded to the family honours, and on the 4th June, 1610, on the occasion of the creation of Henry Prince of Wales, was made a Knight of the Bath, along with twenty-four other lords and gentlemen. In 1623 he was appointed Rear-Admiral of the fleet dis-

* In the *Mirrovr*, only thirteen cross-crosslets are blazoned upon the shield.

patched to Spain for the purpose of bringing home Prince Charles, after his romantic mission with Buckingham to the court of Madrid; on which occasion he entertained the grandees of that court with sumptuous prodigality. Nothing could exceed the splendour of his equipage in this mission, the cost of which, it is said, exceeded £15,000, the whole of which he personally bore, "being of a most free and generous spirit."* Waller has alluded to the reception given the Spaniards by the fleet in a juvenile poem, remarkable to the curious in poetical anecdote, as having been written only twenty-five years after the death of Spenser:—

> "Now had his Highness bid farewell to Spain,
> And reached the sphere of his own power, the main;
> With British bounty in his ship he feasts
> The Hesperian princes, his amazèd guests,
> To find that watery wilderness exceed
> The entertainments of their great Madrid." †

Lord Windsor, who is described as a nobleman of learning and accomplishments, with a taste for antiquities, which he carefully cultivated, married Catharine, daughter of Edward Earl of Worcester, but left no issue. He died in 1642, having bequeathed his whole estate, by special deed, dated December, 1641, to his nephew, Thomas Windsor Hickman, son of Dixie Hickman, Esq., by Elizabeth, his lordship's sister.

THE LORD WENTWORTH, pp. 50, 51.‡

ARMS.—*Sa.*, a chevron between three leopards' faces, *or*, a crescent for difference.

Sir Thomas Wentworth, the great and unfortunate Earl

---

* Banks, vol. ii. p. 612.   † Fenton's *Waller*, Notes, p. 4.
‡ It is worthy of remark that Sir Thomas Wentworth is here styled "The Lord Wentworth," though he was not created a baron—the lowest rank in the British peerage—until 1628, ten years after the *Mirrour* was published; and it is further curious that in the shield assigned him, the badge or distinctive ensign of a baronet, which he was then entitled to bear, is omitted.

of Strafford, was the eldest son of Sir William Wentworth, of Wentworth-Woodhouse, in Yorkshire, the representative of a family founded by Reginald de Winterwade, whose name occurs in Doomsday Book. He was born in Chancery Lane, London, April 13, 1593, and educated at St. John's College, Cambridge; having travelled over the Continent, he returned to England in 1613, when he received the honour of knighthood, and shortly afterwards married Mary, eldest daughter of Francis Clifford, fourth Earl of Cumberland. On the death of his father in the following year, he succeeded to the estates, and also to the baronetcy, which had been conferred by James I., on the original institution of that order, in 1612, and about the same time was returned to Parliament as one of the representatives for Yorkshire, and sat in several successive Parliaments, his leanings being towards the opponents of the court, though without holding extreme views, and in 1615 he was named *custos rotulorum* for the county. In 1626, after the accession of Charles I., he was one of those who were made sheriffs of their counties, to prevent them from sitting in Parliament, a procedure which inspired so much resentment, that he signalized himself by refusing the arbitrary loan exacted in the following year, and suffered imprisonment in consequence.* He returned to the third Parliament of Charles with a feeling of determined opposition to the court, and possibly with some real zeal for the liberties of his country; but, either from ambitious motives or an awakened dread for the safety of the constitution, fearing that his associates were proceeding to too great lengths, he went over to the side of the king, and, to the surprise of all, he was, on the 22nd July, 1628, elevated to the peerage by the title of Baron Wentworth, Newmarsh, and Oversley; thus commencing a splendid and baleful career that ended upon the scaffold.† On the 10th December fol-

* Hallam.
† It is recorded that shortly after his elevation, Strafford met with his old friend Pym, and remarked: "You see, I have left you"; to which the demagogue replied, "So I perceive; but we shall never leave *you* as long as you have a head on your shoulders." Pym kept his word, and never lost sight of Strafford till he had brought him to the block.

lowing he was advanced to the dignity of a viscount, and in the succeeding year made a Privy Councillor, Lord Lieutenant of Yorkshire, and Lord President of the Council of the North, a court possessing inordinate powers, with a criminal jurisdiction extending from the Humber to the Scottish frontier. His love of power being still unsatisfied, he was, in July, 1633, by his own desire, made Lord Deputy of Ireland, a country that had for centuries been the hotbed of faction, and where his commanding energy, his despotic power, and imperious passions created general alarm, and led the way to the rebellion of 1641. In 1640 Strafford received his final honours: on the 12th January he was created Baron Raby, of Raby Castle, in the county of Durham, and Earl of Strafford, and on the 12th September following he was invested with the Order of the Garter. His defection from his friends, his powerful intellect and commanding genius, his steadfast fidelity to his sovereign and to the Church of England, and his lofty and imperious tone in the council-chamber, aroused the fear and hatred of the Parliament party, who were eager to effect his destruction. While with the army in the North, he was apprised by his friends of the gathering storm. In November, 1641, he returned to London, in obedience to the summons of the king, who said he could not dispense with the services of his ablest councillor, receiving the solemn assurance of Charles that, "upon the word of a king, he should not suffer in life, honour, or fortune." * Within a day or two of his arrival he went down to the House, when he was impeached of high treason by the Commons, his former friend, but then sworn adversary, Pym, taking the leading part against him, and the same night he was lodged in the Tower. On the 22nd March, 1641, his trial—one of the most memorable in the annals of the State—began in Westminster Hall, and continued day by day until the 10th April, Strafford defending himself with so much wisdom, eloquence, and ability, that, had he not been foredoomed, his unanswerable arguments must undoubtedly have secured his acquittal. As the impeachment seemed likely to fail,

* Strafford Letters, vol. ii. p. 416.

a bill of attainder was proposed, which was read a first time on the 13th April, and passed on the 21st. Charles, who loved Strafford tenderly, at first refused his assent; but, yielding to the entreaties of those about him, and in violation of the solemn promise he had given, eventually signed the death-warrant, and on the 12th May, 1641, the minister, who had trusted in his promise of protection, was beheaded on Tower Hill, behaving with all that dignity of resolution to be expected from his character. The king's conscience was deeply wounded by his acquiescence in the death of his favourite minister, and he looked back with remorse upon the injustice he had been guilty of during the misfortunes which afterwards overwhelmed him. The political faults of Strafford were doubtless many and great, but the charge of treason was groundless, and the attainder unconstitutional: he was made the victim of popular clamour, and his death was the first political murder. The eulogium of his enemy Whitelock might well serve for his epitaph:—"Thus," he says, "fell this noble earl, who, for natural parts and abilities, and for improvement of knowledge by experience in the greatest affairs—for wisdom, faithfulness, and gallantry of mind, hath left few behind him that can be ranked as his equal."

By his first wife, who died in 1622, Lord Strafford had no issue. On the 24th February, 1625, he married for his second wife Arabella, second daughter of John Holles, first Earl of Clare, a lady of great beauty and cultivated mind, who died in October, 1631, leaving a son, William, and two daughters,—Ann, who married Edward Watson, Earl of Rockingham, and Arabella, who became the wife of John M'Carthy, Viscount Mountcashel. In October, 1632, his lordship again entered the marriage state, his third wife being Elizabeth, daughter of Sir Godfrey Rhodes, Knt., of Great Houghton, in Yorkshire, who bore him two children, Thomas and Margaret, both of whom died unmarried.

In 1662 the attainder of Earl Strafford was reversed, and his eldest son, William, restored to the titles of the house.

THE LORD DARCIE, pp. 52, 53.

ARMS.—*Az.*, semée of cross crosslets, and three cinquefoils, *arg.*

The Lord Dárcie by whom these arms were borne would appear to have been John, the last of the line who bore the title, the only son and heir of Michael Darcy, descended from Norman D'Arcie or D'Areci, who came into England with the Conqueror, and his wife Margaret, daughter of Thomas Wentworth, Esq., and the grandson of John Lord Darcy, restored in blood by the title of Lord Darcy of Aston, 28th August, 1558, who married Agnes, the daughter of Thomas Babington, of Dethick, in the county of Derby, Esq., and sister of Anthony Babington, beheaded for his share in the conspiracy to liberate the Queen of Scots. This John, who served with Walter Earl of Essex in his expedition to Ireland, survived his son Michael, and died in 1587, being succeeded in the title by his grandson John, above named, who married Rosamond, daughter of Sir Peter Frescheville, of Stavely, in Derbyshire, Knt., by whom he had an only son, who pre-deceased him, and two daughters, who both died unmarried.

Lord Darcy dying in 1635 without surviving male issue, the barony ceased, and remained extinct until Charles I., in 1641-2, restored and confirmed it to Sir Conyers Darcy, Knt., the grandson of Arthur, younger brother of John Lord Darcy, restored in blood, and the son of Thomas Lord Darcy, who was beheaded in the reign of Henry VIII.

Contemporaneous with the Lord Darcy of Aston, above mentioned, there was a Lord Darcy of Chiche, in Essex. Thomas, the third baron, eldest son of John Lord Darcy (who also claimed descent from Norman D'Arcie), by Frances, daughter of Richard Lord Rich, which Thomas, on the 5th July, 1621, was created by James I. Viscount Colchester, with limitation, on failure of male issue, to his son-in-law, Sir Thomas Savage, of Rock-Savage, in Cheshire,

ARMS AND PERSONAGES. 149

and the heirs of his body by Elizabeth his wife, eldest daughter of Lord Thomas; and on the 4th November, 2 Charles I. (1626), was further advanced to the earldom of Rivers, with like limitation. His lordship died February 21, 1639, and having survived his only son, Thomas, who died issueless, the barony of Chiche failed; but the titles of Colchester and Rivers devolved upon his son-in-law, Sir Thomas Savage, in accordance with the limitation named.

The arms borne by Lord Darcy of Chiche—*arg.*, three cinquefoils, *gu.*—differ from those depicted in the *Mirrour of Maiestie*, and we may therefore assume that Lord Darcy of Aston was the "noble personage rancked in the Catalogue."

THE LORD WOTTON, pp. 54, 55.

ARMS.—*Arg.*, a cross formée, fitchée at the foot, *sa.*

Sir Edward Wotton, Lord Wotton of Marley, was the eldest son of Thomas Wotton, of Boughton Malherbe, in the county of Kent, and the brother of Sir Henry Wotton, Lord Essex's secretary (the famous diplomatist and political writer), of Sir James, who distinguished himself in the expedition to Cadiz, and of Sir John, the accomplished scholar and traveller. Sir Edward having been introduced at court, was knighted by Queen Elizabeth and made Comptroller of her Majesty's Household, and was, says Camden, "remarkable for many and great employments in the State during her reign, and sent several times ambassador into foreign nations." After the accession of James, he was, on the 20th May, 1603, made a baron of the realm by the title of Lord Wotton of Marley, in the county of Kent; Sir Robert Sidney of Penshurst, Sir William Knollys, and Sir Robert Cecil being elevated to the peerage at the same time; and on the 22nd December, 1616, he was appointed Treasurer of the King's Household, but surrendered his staff of office on the 1st February,

1618. Like the rest of his family, Lord Wotton was conspicuous for his refined taste and mental qualifications. He married Esther, daughter and coheir of Sir William Puckering, of Yorkshire, Knt., and by her had issue an only son, Thomas, born in 1597, who succeeded him, and died in 1630.

THE LORD STANHOPE, pp. 56, 57.

ARMS.—Quarterly, *erm.* and *gu.*

John Stanhope, Lord Stanhope of Harrington, was the third son of Sir Michael Stanhope, of Shelford, in Nottinghamshire, who was beheaded in 1552 with Sir Thomas Arundel, for conspiring the death of Dudley, Duke of Northumberland, his mother being Ann, daughter of Nicholas Rawson, Esq., of Aveley Bellhouse, in Essex. During the reign of Elizabeth and James, he was in much favour at court, and held several important offices, including those of Treasurer of the Chambers and Master of the Ports. On the 4th May, 1605, being then Vice-Chamberlain to the king, he was raised to the peerage by the title of Baron Stanhope of Harrington, being the first of this house, though of ancient and honourable descent, that was ennobled. His lordship died 9th March, 1620, having had issue by his wife Margaret, daughter and coheir of Henry M'Williams, of Stanbourne, in Essex, two daughters, viz., Elizabeth, married to Sir Lionel Tollemache, father of the first Earl of Dysart, and Catharine, married to Robert Cholmondeley, created in 1628 Viscount Cholmondeley, and an only son, Charles, who succeeded, as second Lord Stanhope, and, having married Dorothy, sister to the Earl of Newburgh, died issueless in 1677, when the dignity expired.

THE LORD CAREVV, pp. 58, 59.

ARMS.—*Or*, three lioncels, passant in pale, *sa.*, armed and langued, *gu.*: a crescent for difference.

This distinguished soldier, George Lord Carew, of Clopton, in the county of Warwick, was the son of George Carew, Archdeacon of Totness and Dean of Exeter, descended from Sir Thomas Carew, who served with distinction at the battle of Agincourt. He was born in 1557, and at the age of fifteen began his academical career at Broad-gate Hall (now Pembroke College), Oxford, where he attained considerable proficiency. On quitting the university, he embraced the profession of arms, and served in the Irish wars against the Earl of Desmond and other rebels. In 1580 he was made Governor of the Castle of Askeaton, and some years later was appointed Lieutenant-General of Artillery, and Master of the Ordnance in Ireland. In 1596 he was nominated to a command in the expedition fitted out to destroy the Spanish fleet in the port of Cadiz, and on the 19th February, 1598, he accompanied Secretary Cecil as ambassador to France, from which country he returned 1st May following; in the succeeding year he was appointed Lord President of Munster, and in 1600 made Treasurer of the Army, and also one of the Lords Justices of Ireland, that country at the time being in a state of open rebellion, whilst the entire force at his disposal for its suppression numbered only 3,000 infantry and 250 cavalry. By his consummate skill and valour he overcame all difficulties; he made the Earl of Desmond and the chieftain O'Connor prisoners, brought the other rebel chiefs under subjection, and reduced all the fortified strongholds. In 1601 he defeated a body of Spaniards who had landed at Kinsale, and the next year attacked and captured the castle of Dunboy, until then deemed impregnable; thereby preventing another projected invasion, which the Spaniards abandoned on hearing of the fall of that stronghold. In 1603, Elizabeth having reluctantly accepted the resignation of his burdensome office, he returned to England, arriving only three days before the queen's death. By her successor his merits were highly valued. On the 2nd May, 1603, he was deputed by the Lords of the Council, with other distinguished personages, to attend Ann, queen of James I., on her journey from Scotland into England. In the same year he was appointed Governor of Guernsey, and on the 4th June, 1605, was created a peer of the realm, by the title of Baron Carew of Clopton, in the county of Warwick. In 1608 he was appointed Master-General of Ordnance of Great Britain; on the 20th July, 1616, sworn of the Privy Council; and in 1625, on the accession of Charles I., he was raised to the earldom of Totness, a dignity he enjoyed only four years, his death occurring at the Savoy, London, 1629, in the seventy-second year of his age.

THE LORD HAYE, pp. 60, 61.

ARMS.—*Arg.*, three escutcheons, *gu.*

James Lord Hay, the frivolous fantastic spendthrift, who in the reign of James I. shared so large a portion of the royal favour and the royal purse, was the son of a Scottish merchant. He received his education in France, and returning to England about the time of James's accession, was presented at court by the French ambassador, where his showy person and elegance of manners quickly rendered him a favourite. On the 29th June, 1615, he was ennobled by the title of Lord Hay of Sawley, a creation that would seem to have originated in some freak of the king, the dignity being conferred without the issue of letters-patent or a seat in the House of Lords. In 1616 he was sent on a mission to Paris to congratulate the king of France on his marriage with the

Infanta of Spain, and to ask the hand of the Princess Christian, eldest daughter of Louis XIII., for the Prince Charles. Nothing could exceed the splendour of this embassage; the members of his train were clothed in the most costly liveries, and the horse on which he rode was shod with silver shoes lightly tacked on, so that they could be flung away for the greedy bystanders to scramble for, a farrier or *argentier* following with others, which were scattered about with the same extravagant prodigality.* On the 20th March, 1617, he was sworn of the Privy Council, and on the 5th July in the following year raised to the title of Viscount Doncaster. In 1619 he was sent ambassador to Germany, with a view of mediating between the emperor and the Bohemians, a mission that is estimated to have cost no less than fifty or sixty thousand pounds. In 1621 he was sent upon another embassage to France, to mediate between Louis XIII. and the French Protestants, but his diplomacy was not attended with success. In September, 1622, he was raised to the earldom of Carlisle, and in the following year he was at Madrid during the matrimonial visit of Prince Charles, though there is no evidence of his being employed officially. After the accession of Charles I., he does not appear to have held any very important office, though he was not entirely overlooked, being in 1633 named first gentleman† of the bedchamber to the king. His death occurred April 25, 1636, when, says Clarendon, he left neither "a house nor an acre of land to be remembered by," a statement that is contradicted by Lodge, who affirms that, "notwithstanding his expensive absurdities, he left a very large fortune, partly derived from his marriage with the heiress of the Lords Denny, but more from the king's unlimited bounty." The earl carefully shunned politics, which would have made him enemies; and thus he escaped the fate of Somerset, Buckingham, and Strafford. If he was prodigal

---

* Wilson, p. 94.
† Formerly the title of "gentleman" implied, in its strictest sense, nobility.

in his expenditure, it was in accordance with the tastes of his sovereign, whose character he understood more thoroughly perhaps than any of his contemporaries. With all his failings, he was modest and unassuming, and his unaffected courtesy and generous hospitality made him a general favourite—"he was a sensualist without being selfish, and a courtier without being insolent."

The earl married, first, Honora, sole daughter and heir of Edward Lord Denny, afterwards created Earl of Norwich. Surviving her, he married, secondly, November 6, 1617, the beautiful but frivolous Lady Lucy Percy, youngest daughter of Henry, eighth Earl of Northumberland, the most enchanting woman at the court of Charles, and, next to the far-famed Sacharissa, the goddess of Waller's idolatry.

THE LORD CHIEFE IUSTICE OF THE KINGS-BENCH, pp. 62, 63.

ARMS.—*Arg.*, three lozenges, conjoined, in fesse, *gu.*, within a bordure, *sa.*, differenced by a mullet, the mark of cadency of a third son.

This distinguished lawyer and parliamentary orator, Sir Henry Montagu, the founder of the ducal house of Manchester, was the third of the six sons of Sir Edward Montagu, by Elizabeth, daughter of Sir James Harington, of Exton, in Rutlandshire, and the grandson of Sir Edward Montagu, Lord Chief Justice of the King's Bench in 1539. On the 23rd July, 1603, he was knighted by James I. at Westminster, along with some three or four hundred others; on the 19th March, 1604, he was returned as representative of the City of London in the first Parliament of James; on the 18th November, 1616, he was sworn Lord Chief Justice of the King's Bench; on Monday, December 4, 1620, he was made Lord Treasurer of England at Newmarket, where the king

ARMS AND PERSONAGES.   155

gave him his staff and created him Lord Montagu, Baron of Kimbolton and Viscount Mandeville; and on Saturday, the 16th of the same month, he was sworn at the Exchequer. On the accession of Charles I., he was created Earl of Manchester (February 5, 1626), and was afterwards appointed Lord Privy Seal. The earl was thrice married; first, to Catharine, second daughter of Sir William Spencer, of Yarnton, in Oxfordshire, by whom he had three sons; secondly, to Ann, daughter and heir of William Wincot, Esq., of Langham, in Staffordshire, and widow of Sir Leonard Halliday, Knt., Lord Mayor of London, but by her had no issue; his third wife, whom he married in 1620, being Margaret, daughter of John Crouch, Esq., of Cornbury, in Hertfordshire, and widow of John Hare, Esq., who bore him a son, George Montagu, ancestor of the Earls of Halifax, and a daughter, Susannah, who became the wife of George Brydges, sixth Lord Chandos. His lordship died November 6, 1642, and was succeeded in the title by his eldest son, Edward Montagu, the renowned parliamentarian general, who defeated Prince Rupert at Marston Moor, when Cromwell acted as his lieutenant-general, and who at the Restoration was accepted by the Lords as their speaker to congratulate Charles II. on his return to his capital.

THE LORD CHIEFE IUSTICE OF THE COMMON-PLEAS, pp. 62, 63.

ARMS.—*Sa.*, an estoile of eight * points, *or*, between two flaunches, *erm.*, differenced by a crescent.

Sir Henry Hobart, by whom this coat was borne, was the second son of Miles Hobart, of Plumstede, by Audrey, daughter and coheir of William Hare, Esq., of Beeston, in Norfolk. Having completed his education, he adopted

---

* In the shield depicted in the *Mirrour*, the estoile has only six points.

the profession of the law, and soon rose to considerable eminence. In 1595 he was chosen steward of the city of Norwich, and in the following year elected one of the governors of his own inn, being about the same time returned burgess in Parliament for Yarmouth, which borough he also represented in 1600. In 1603 he was called to the degree of serjeant-at-law, and on the 23rd July in the same year he received the honour of knighthood, in company with his eldest son, John. He represented the city of Norwich in the first Parliament of James I., and, being held in high repute for his ability and learning, was in 1605 made attorney to the Court of Wards, and on the 4th July of the same year constituted King's Attorney-General. On the 22nd July, 1610, he was appointed by letters patent one of the first governors of the Charter-house,* and on the 22nd November in the following year created a baronet, being the ninth in precedency in the institution of that order. On the 26th October, 1613, he was appointed successor to Sir Edward Coke as Lord Chief Justice of the Common Pleas, an office in which he acquitted himself with much honour, Sir Francis Bacon being at the same time constituted Attorney-General. Bacon was his rival, and, in 1615, on the anticipated death of Lord Chancellor Ellesmere, fearing that Sir Henry Hobart might be appointed to succeed, he addressed a letter to the king, under date 12th February, 1615, "touching the Lord Chancellor's place," in which occurs the following passage:—

"If you take my Lord Hubbard [Hobart], you shall have a judge at the upper end of your council-board and another [Coke] at the lower end, whereby your Majesty will find your prerogative pent; for though there should be emulation between them, yet, as legists, they will agree in magnifying that wherein they are best. He is no statesman, but an œconomist, wholly for himself; so as your Majesty, more than an outward form, will find little help in him for your business."†

In the later years of his life he commenced the rebuilding

* Stow, 940.
† Lambeth MSS. quoted in Spedding's *Letters and Life of Francis Bacon*, ed. 1869.

ARMS AND PERSONAGES. 157

of Blickling Hall,* one of the most perfect examples remaining of the time of the first James, previously the seat of the Boleyns, and celebrated as the house from which Henry VIII. married the ill-fated mother of Queen Elizabeth, the Lady Anne Boleyn. At his decease were published reports of several law cases, which bear this title: *The Reports of that Reverend and Learned Judge, the Right Hon. Sir Henry Hobart, Knt. and Bart., Lord Chief Justice of His Majesty's Court of Common Pleas, and Chancellor to both their Highnesses, Henry and Charles, Prince of Wales,* &c. On the 22nd April, 1590, he married, at Blickling, Dorothy, daughter of Sir Robert Bell, of Beaupre Hall, in Norfolk, Knt., Lord Chief Baron of the Exchequer, by whom he had sixteen children, one of them being Sir Miles Hobart, noted in the time of Charles I. for his opposition to the royalist party, and who, on the 2nd March, 1628-9, to prevent the anticipated dissolution of Parliament, forcibly held the Speaker, Sir John Finch, in the chair while certain strong resolutions were passed.

Sir Henry Hobart died December 26, 1625, and was succeeded by his eldest son, Sir John Hobart, who married, first, Philippa, daughter of Robert Sidney, Earl of Leicester, and, secondly, Frances, eldest daughter of John Earl of Bridgewater; but, dying without surviving male issue, the title devolved upon his nephew, Sir John Hobart, grandfather of the first Earl of Buckinghamshire.

THE LORD CHIEFE BARON OF THE EXCHEAQUER, pp. 62, 63.

ARMS.—*Arg.*, two chevrons between three martlets, *sa.*, two and one.

Sir Laurence Tanfield, Lord Chief Baron of the Exchequer, the last of the "personages rancked in the Catalogue," was

---

* Mr. Henry Shaw, F.S.A., remarks that the entrance-porch to this stately mansion "may be regarded as one of the earliest attempts at the restoration of classical architecture, and appears to be formed upon the model of the Arch of Titus at Rome."

the only son of Robert Tanfield, of Burford, in Oxfordshire, by his wife, Wilgeford Fitzherbert, and the third in descent from Robert Tanfield, the representative of a family seated at Harpole and Gayton, in Northamptonshire, from the time of Henry VI. This Robert Tanfield married Catharine, daughter of Edward Neville, Baron Abergavenny, by his second wife, Catharine, sister of John Howard, Duke of Norfolk. Laurence Tanfield's name occurs as Reader of the Society of the Inner Temple in 1595; on the 10th January, 1605, he was appointed a puisne justice of the King's Bench, and on the 25th June, 1607, created Lord Chief Baron of the Exchequer, in the place of Sir Thomas Fleming, who had been made Chief Justice of the King's Bench; and this dignity he held during the remainder of his life. He died on the 30th April, 1625, and was buried in the church of Burford, his native place, in which, in the centre of an enclosed aisle or chapel on the north side of the church, is an altar-tomb, with the recumbent effigies of himself and his wife beneath an enriched canopy, supported by ornamental pillars. By his wife Elizabeth, daughter of Gyles Symonds, of Cley, in Norfolk, he had issue an only daughter, bearing the same baptismal name as her mother, who became the wife of Sir Henry Cary, K.B., created Viscount Falkland November 10, 1620, whose son Lucius, the second viscount, born in 1610,—"Falkland the generous and the just,"—became heir to his maternal grandfather, and lost his life at the battle of Newbury, September 20, 1643, whilst fighting on the royalist side.

J. C.

III.

NOTICE OF WORKS WITH SIMILAR TITLES, AND ESPECIALLY OF THOSE WHICH CONTAIN THE ILLUSTRATIVE PLATES.

WERE we to bring together into a regular series full notices of the various works in literature which bear on their title-pages the English word *Mirror*, or the French *Miroir*, the German and Dutch 𝔖𝔭𝔦𝔢𝔤𝔢𝔩, the Latin *Speculum*, and the Greek *Theatron*, we should have to compile a volume, rather than a chapter. The subjects, too, treated of would be found almost universal. Though in its exercise often doing violence to good taste, and at times offending against the proprieties of thought, the idea has for centuries been popular of holding up a glass and of looking within it to see reflected characters, personages, events, histories, moral instruction, philosophical, spiritual, and religious truths, and the whole contour of society, of government, and of the world.

It is a long time ago, too, since the use of jingling alliterative titles became prevalent. Not to travel out of our English tongue, nor away from the one word Mirror, we may refer to a curious medley of subjects, all set forth in the looking-glass of the imagination, and imprinted for the edification of mankind. Thus :—

"THE MIRROURE of Gold for the synfull soule, translated out of frenche into englishe by the right excellent princesse Margaret moder to our soueraigne lord king Henry the VII." London, *Pynson*. 4to.

"A MYRROUR FOR MAN"; by Tho. Churchyard, *about* 1550.

"THE MIRROUR of Madnes, or a Paradoxe maintayning Madness to be most excellent"; by J. Sandford. 8vo. LONDON. 1576.

WORKS WITH SIMILAR TITLES.

"A MIRRHOR mete for all Mothers, Matrones and Maidens, entituled the Mirrhor of Modestie";—"A pretie and pithie Dialogue betweene Mercurie and Virtue"; by Thomas Salter. 8vo. London. 1579.

"THE MIRROUR of Mutabilitie, or principall part of the Mirrour for Magistrates"; by Antony Munday. 4to. London. 1579.

"A MIROUR of Monsters"; compiled by W. Rankins, A.D. 1587.

"THE MIRROR of Martyrs; the life and death of that thrice valient Capitaine, and most godly Martyre, Sir John Old-castle knight Lord Cobham"; by John Weever. 8vo. 1601.

But, above them all, we name and commend

"A MIROVR FOR MAGISTRATES,* being a true Chronicle Historie of the vntimely falles of such vnfortunate Princes and men of note, as haue happened since the first entrance of Brute into this Iland, vntill this our latter Age. *Newly enlarged with a last part*, called, *A Winter-night's Vision*,† being an addition of such Tragedies, especially famous, as are exampled in this former Historie, with a Poem annexed called *England's Eliza*." (The Device is a wand entwined by two serpents, two cornucopiæ, hands issuing from clouds, and the motto "By Peace Plenty, by Wisdom Peace.") "At London, Imprinted by Felix Kyngstun 1610." 8vo. Pages, 20 unnumbered, 1—875 numbered.

This work, commenced in 1559, was added to at various times, until from less than thirty tales, or histories, it was enlarged so as to comprise eighty legends and eleven supplements. In the entire volume the first legend tells, "How King *Albanuet* the yongest sonne of Brutus and first King of Albanie (now called Scotland) was slain by *King Humber, the yeare before Christ* 1085"; and the eightieth records, "How the *Lord Cromwell* exalted from meane estate was after by the enuie of the Bishop of Winchester and other his complices brought to vntimely end Anno Dom. 1540." Of the *eleven* additions, the eighty-first tale gives "The life and death of King Arthur"; and the ninety-first the poem annexed, *England's Eliza*, p. 873, of which the following is a stanza:—

---

* "*The Induction*" to the work was composed by the celebrated Thomas Sackville, Earl of Dorset, in 1563. To him also is assigned "*The Complaint of the Duke of Buckingham.*" Thomas Sackville died in 1608, leaving behind a very memorable name.

† This *Winter-night's Vision* was dedicated to Charles Howard, the Earl of Nottingham, who was "the Lord Admirall" of the *Mirrovr of Maiestie*, pp. 19, 20.

MIRRORS.

> "Thus to the life of our triumphant Dame
> Time in her reigne no yeere did multiplie
> Which Fortune did not dignyfie with fame
> Or praise of some illustrate victorie;
> 'Gainst Rome, 'gainst Spaine, or th' Austrian enemie
> 'Gainst whom that houre that she expir'd her breath,
> She di'd victorious in the armes of death."

With the unalliterative titles our array might easily be swelled out, but not to so great a degree as might be imagined. *The Myrrour of the worlde* appeared in 1481, and Fewterer's *Myrrour* or *Glasse of Christis Passion* in 1534. The *Mirrour of Princely deeds* is dated 1579; Robert Greene's *Mirrour or looking glasse for the Ladies of England*, 4to, 1583; and the same author's " *Penelope's Web*, Wherein a Christall Myrror of fœminine perfection repteseents to the viewe of euery those vertues and graces, which more curiously beautifies the mynd of women, then eyther sumptuous Apparell, or Iewels of inestimable valew." 4to. 1587.

The *Mariners Mirror* became known in 1583; and in 1594 Drayton's *Ideas Mirrour*, or love stanzas, of fourteen lines each; and in the early part of the reign of King James, 1604, the "*Mirrour of his Maiesties present Gouernment* tending to the Vnion of his whole Iland of Brittone."

For showing the variety of subjects in French works that glorify themselves in the word *Miroir*, it will be sufficient to specify two or three :—

"Guguin's MIROUER historial de France," a folio of 185 leaves, printed in 1516. It is from the author's Latin chronicles of an earlier date, 1499, and contains the deeds and actions of kings of France.
"MIRROUER des femmes vertueuses," à Lyon, 1546; a very rare volume, containing the Patience of Griselda, and the History of the Maid of Orleans.
"LE MIROIR des escoliers et de la jeunesse." 8vo. 1602.

Glass and *Looking-glass* also furnish their full quota of titles. In 1590 there was a *Looking-glass for England*, and in 1599 another *for Ireland*. A *Glasse for Gamesters* was printed in 1581; and in 1589 a *Spectacle for Perjurers*, adorned in the title-page with the circles of a pair of spectacles. The French, too, at a much earlier day, had their

Lunettes to give point to a title; for "*Les lunettes des princes*," by Jehan Meschinot, dates from Nantes, in small 4to, 1493, and through above twenty editions retained its popularity to 1539. The word reappeared at Orleans in 1576, when "*Lunettes de christal de roche*" were recommended to all the princes, lords, gentlemen, and other good Frenchmen, to enable them to see clearly the way by which it was sought to bring France under the same tyranny as Turkey.

A work far more truly a Mirror of Majesty than the trifling volume which expressly bears the name, is Henry Holland's BOOKE OF KINGS, also printed A.D. 1618: it is a folio with thirty-two noble plates, chiefly the workmanship of Reginald Elstracke, an English engraver, and of Simon, the brother of Crispin de Passe the younger. This Simon de Passe resided in England about ten years, from 1613, and then engaged in the service of the King of Denmark. The title of the *Book of Kings* and the portrait of William the Conqueror,* were engraved by Elstracke, and the fine portraits of Elizabeth, James, and Anna, by Simon de Passe, to whom also are to be attributed several other portraits of eminent men of their day. This ΒΑΖΙΛΙΩΛΟΓΙΑ is well described by its title.

"A BOOKE OF KINGS, beeing the true and liuely Effigies of all our English Kings from the Conquest vntill this present: With their seuerall Coats of Arms, Impreses, and Devises. And a briefe Chronologie of their Liues and Deaths elegantly grauen in copper. (London) Printed for H. Holland and are to be sold by Compton Holland over against the Exchange. 1618." Small fo.io.

Of the thirty-two portraits in the *Book of Kings*, there are only three of the personages named in the *Mirrovr of Maiestie:* they are "James, King of Great Britaine," Anna his queen, and "Charles, Prince of great Britaine and Ireland." † But with the *Basiliωlogia* proper are sometimes found additional portraits; as, Edward Somerset,

---

* See Bryan's *Dictionary of Engravers and Painters*, 1849, p. 229.
† See *Mirrovr of Maiestie*, pp. 1, 4, and 6.

BOOKS OF PORTRAITS. 163

Earl of Worcester, "the Lord Privy Seale," and Henry Wriothesley, "Earle of Southampton."*

A most worthy companion to Holland's *Booke of Kings* was his *Book of Heroes*.

"HERωOLOGIA ANGLICA, hoc est clarissimorvm et doctissimorvm aliqvot Anglorvm, qvi florvervnt ab Anno Cristi M.D. vsq. ad presentem Annvm M.D.C.XX. viuæ Effigies, Vitæ et Elogia, duobus Tomis. Authore H. H. Anglo Britanno. Impensis Crispini Passæi Calcographus et Jansonij Bibliopolæ Arnhemiensis." Folio.

The work contains sixty-five portraits attributed to Crispin de Passe the elder, his son William de Passe, and others. A few of the originals were by Hans Holbein, and one or two by Rubens. Of persons commemorated in the *Mirrovr of Maiestie*, there are three portraits in the *Booke of Heroes;* of William Herbert, Earl of Pembroke, ".the Lord Chamberline"; Robert Devereux, "the Earle of Essex," and James Montagu, "the Bishop of Winchester."†

Several works of later times supply authentic portraits and memoirs of the "Noble Personages rancked in the Catalogue" of our fac-simile Reprint. We select the following, to which our readers are referred :—

Clarendon's *History of the Rebellion and Civil Wars in England;* 8vo, 3 vols. in 6, with Portraits forming a 7th part. Oxford. Printed at the Theater, An. Dom. MDCCVII.

Birch's *Heads of Illustrious Persons of Great Britain*, engraven by Mr. Houbraken and Mr. Vertue, with their Lives and Characters. Large folio, 2 vols. London, MDCCXLIII.

Thane's (or Daniel's) *British Autobiography*. A Collection of Fac-similes of Hand-writing of royal and illustrious Personages, with their authentic Portraits. 4to. London, 1788 and 1839.

Granger's *Biographical History of England*, Portraits Illustrative of. 4to. London, 1799.

Lodge's *Portraits of Illustrious Personages of Great Britain*, engraved from authentic Pictures in the Galleries of the Nobility and the Public Collections of the Country, with biographical and historical Memoirs of their Lives and Actions. Folio, 4 vols. 240 plates. London, 1821—1834.

---

* See *Mirrovr of Maiestie*, pp. 14 and 26. † *Id.*, pp. 22, 30, and 42.

For identifying several of the ministers of State and other illustrious men named in the *Mirrovr of Maiestie*, we have found an heraldic work very serviceable, which was printed four years later, in 1622. It is a small folio of 392 pages, and was dedicated "TO THE HIGH AND MIGHTY PRINCE JAMES, King of Great Britaine, France and Ireland, &c." Of English kings are emblazoned twenty coats of arms, and of the nobles about 655. There are also notices of the various persons whose insignia are represented. The title alone may serve to set forth what an intimate reference the book bears to the *Mirrovr* of King James's *Maiestie*.

"A CATALOGUE and succession of the *Kings, Princes, Dukes,* Marquesses, Earles, and Viscounts of this Realme of England since *the Norman Conquest* to this present yeere 1622. Together with their Armes, *Wiues and Children, the times of their Deaths* and Burials, with many of their memorable Actions. *Collected by* RALPH BROOKE, *Esquire, Yorke Herauld, and by him enlarged,* with amendment of diuers faults, committed by the *Printer,* in *the time* of the Authors sicknesse. *Quamquisq; norit artem, in hac se exerceat.*"*

A volume very similar in nature to the last, and serving the same purpose, though rather later in time, has the following title set within a monumental border.

"THE VNION OF HONOVR containing the armes, Matches and Issues of the Kings, Dukes, Marquesses and Earles of England from the Conquest untill this present yeare 1641. With the Armes of the English Viscounts and Barons now being; and of the Gentry of Lincolnister. Whereunto is annexed A briefe of all the Battels which have beene fought and maintained by the English since the Conquest, till the yeare 1602. Collected out of the most approued Authours former or moderne. By James Yorke, Black-Smith.
"London, Printed by *Edward Griffin* for WILLIAM LECKE, and are to be sold at his Shop in *Chancery-lane* neare unto the Rolls. 1640." Folio.

For comparison with the Royal Arms of James and of his queen, as presented in the *Mirrovr*, pp. 1 and 4, we have

---

* Prefixed to the copy made use of (belonging to Lee P. Townshend, Esq., of Wincham Hall, Cheshire), is an exquisite "*Portraiture of the illustrious* Princesse Frances Duchess *of* Richmond *and* Lenox;" Anno 1623, *insculptum a Guilh. Passæo Londinium.* The noble lady was daughter of Thomas Lord Howard of Bindon, and wife of Ludowick Stuart, Duke of Lennox. See *Mirrovr of Maiestie,* p. 18, Emb. 10.

consulted the magnificent folio which bears on the reverse of the title-page the treble mottoes, "*Gang forword*," "*I am ready*," and "FAX MENTIS HONESTÆ GLORIA"— "*Glory is the torch of the honourable mind;*" where the lines may be applied, first written concerning the lilies, "*beautious flowres*," on the shield of Ludowick Stuart,*—

> "These golden Buckles bordring them about,
> A Palizado, to keepe Foulenesse out."

"Examples of the Ornamental HERALDRY *of the* SIXTEENH CENTVRY. LONDON MDCCCLXVII." Parts I. and II.

The *Royal Arms* of Scotland, Edinburgh, *circa* 1542, *Jacobvs* being *Rex*, are presented in Part II. p. 8; and Edinburgh, 1566, *Maria Regina*, p. 22; the *Royal Arms* of Denmark and *Ducal Arms* of Holstein, Hamburgh, 1590, p. 28; and the *Royal Arms* of Scotland, *impaled with those* of Denmark, Edinburgh, 1593; the motto, *In my defenc, God me defend*, p. 31.

In the same work there are also *two* other plates of considerable interest: the *one*, in Part I. p. 55, bearing on the claim of James to the English throne, 1587; and the *other*, dated 1597, in Part II. p. 82, presenting well-executed portraits of JACOBVS SEXTVS, of his son HENRICVS, and of ANNA REGINA. The side ornamentation, moreover, contains portraits of the sovereigns of Scotland,—IACOBVS PRIMVS, IACOBVS SECVNDVS, IACOBVS TERTIVS, IACOBVS QVARTVS, IACOBVS QVINTVS, and MARIA REGINA.

1. Within a border of the Royal Arms of England, France, Scotland, and their dependencies, is the title in French of a book first published in Latin in 1578 :—

"DV DROICT ET TILTRE de la Serenissime Princesse Marie Royne d'Escosse, et de tres illustre princ Iaques VI. Roy d'Escosse son fils, à la succession du Royaume d'Angleterre. *Auec la genealogie des Roys d'Angleterre ayans regné depuis cinq cens ans.* Premierement composé en Latin & Anglois, par R. P. en Dieu M. Iean de Lesselie Euesque de Rosse, Escossois, lors qu'il estoit Ambassadeur en Angleterre pour sa Majesté, & nouellement mis en François par le mesme Autheur."
A ROVEN De l'Imprimerie de George l'Oyselet. (1587.)

---

* See *Mirrovr of Maiestie*, p. 18.

2. Within a border of portraits of Scottish sovereigns and of the Royal Arms of Scotland, in combination with those of the city of Edinburgh, is the following title :—

"THE LAWES AND ACTES OF PARLIAMENT, maid be King Iames the first and his Svccessovrs, *Kings of Scotlād: visied, collected and extracted furth of the Register.* The Contents of this Bvik ar expreemtd in the leafe following.
"EDINBVRGH Printed by Robert Waldegrave, Printer to the Kings Majestie. 15 Martii A.D. 1597."

From the several works which have thus, in pages 162 to 166, been briefly noticed, PORTRAITS or MEMOIRS may be obtained of a large proportion of the persons named in the *Mirrovr of Maiestie.* We refer to them in the order of the Arms and Emblems, adding the names of the authors where particulars may be found. The necessary limits of our edition render their reproduction in these pages impossible :—

The Kings Maiestie, p. 1, EMB. 2. *See* Holland, Clarendon, Thane, Granger.
The Queene, p. 4, EMB. 3. Holland, Birch, Granger.
The Prince, p. 6, EMB. 4. Holland, Clarendon, Granger.
The Lord Arch-bishop of Canterburie, George Abbott, p. 8, EMB. 5. Clarendon, Birch, Granger. Lodge.
The Lord Chancellor, F. Bacon, p. 10, EMB. 6. Clarendon, Birch, Thane, Lodge.
The Lord Treasurer, Thomas Howard, p. 12, EMB. 7. Thane, Granger, Lodge.
The Lord Priuie Seale, Edward Somerset, p. 14, EMB. 8. Holland.
The Lord Admirall, Charles Howard, p. 16, EMB. 9. Granger.
The Duke of Lenox, Lodowick Stuart, p. 18, EMB. 10. Thane, Granger, Lodge.
The Marquesse of Buckinghame, George Villiers, p. 20, EMB. 11. Clarendon, Birch, Thane, Lodge.
The Lord Chamberlaine, William Herbert, p. 22, EMB. 12. Holland, Clarendon, Lodge.
The Earle of Arundell, Thomas Howard, p. 24, EMB. 13. Clarendon, Thane, Lodge.
The Earle of Southehampton, Henry Wriothesley, p. 26, EMB. 14. Holland, Granger, Lodge.
The Earle of Hertford, Edward Seymour, p. 28, EMB. 15.
The Earle of Essex, Robert Devereux, p. 30, EMB. 16. Holland, Clarendon, Thane, Granger, Lodge.
The Earle of Mountgomerie, Philip Herbert, p. 34, EMB. 18. Clarendon, Granger, Lodge.
The Viscount Wallingford, William Knolles, p. 38, EMB. 20. Granger.

The Bishop of London, John King, p. 40, EMB. 21. Granger.
The Bishop of Winchester, James Montagu, p. 42, EMB. 22. Holland's Herowlogia, Granger.
The Bishop of Ely, Lancelot Andrews, p. 44, EMB. 23. Granger.
The Lord Zouch, Edward la Zouch, p. 46, EMB. 24. Granger.
The Lord Chiefe Iustice of the Kings Bench, Sir Henry Montagu, p. 62, EMB. 32. Granger

The THIRTY-TWO EMBLEMS in the work have no great degree of originality, nor of skilfulness in the design, but, on the whole, if not well executed, are adapted to the noble personages to whom they are addressed. From the practice of the age in which the *Mirrovr of Maiestie* was written, we must expect to meet with occasional, if not with gross, flatteries; these are evident enough, and but little adorned by elegance of diction or refinement of thought. The devices themselves, however, are generally clearly described, —and occasionally the character is very justly set forth, as in the case of Thomas Howard, the Earl of Arundel, whose symbols are the sun and a fruitful tree, that is standing on a hill (p. 27).

> " Know (honour'd Sir) that th' heate of Princes loue,
> Throw'n on those reall *Worths*, good men approue
> Doth, like the radiant *Phœbus* shining here,
> Make fruitfull vertue at full height appeare:
> T" illustrate this in you, were to confesse
> How much your *Goodnesse* doth your *Greatnesse* blesse,
> By its own warme reflexe: thus both suruiue,
> And both i' th *Sunne* of *Royal fauour* thriue
> O may's reuerberating rayes still nourish
> Your noble *Worths*, and make your *Vertues* flourish."

The MOTTOES, in alphabetical order, and the subjects of their DEVICES, we now subjoin:—

BIS INTERIMITVR QVI SVIS ARMIS PERIT—*Twice is he slain who perishes with his arms*, p. 51, Emb. 29. The assailants of Christ's citadel perishing in their own fires.
CANDIDA, SOLIDA, ET IMMOBILE*—*Pure, constant, and immovable*, p. 23, Emb. 12. Piety clasping Alethea's pillar.
CHIARO QVIETO PROFONDO E DIVINO — *Clear, peaceful, deep, and divine*, p. 47, Emb. 24. Phœbus and the sacred Sisters at the Thespian spring.

---

* The incorrect Latin must sometimes be forgiven.

WORKS WITH SIMILAR TITLES.

D' ODORE IL MONDO E D' ACVTEZZA IL CIELO—*The world by sweetness, and the heavens by sharpness*, p. 33, Emb. 17. The fir-tree.

ET DEO ET PATRIÆ—*Both for God and for Country*, p. 15, Emb. 8. A sword and mailed hand on a burning altar.

ET TENEBRÆ FACTÆ SVNT—*And darkness arose*, p. 53, Emb. 27. Black clouds gathered over an eagle.

IN VTRAQVE PERFECTVS—*Made perfect for both offices*, p. 27, Emb. 14. A figure half Mars and half Mercury.

INVIDIA SVVM TORQVET AVTHOREM—*Envy torments its own author*, p. 21, Emb. 11. The envious hand drawing to itself fires from the sun.

IOVIS, APOLLINIS ET MINERVÆ—*Jove's, Apollo's, and Minerva's temple*, p. 51, Emb. 26. Statues of Jupiter, Apollo, and Minerva.

MERITVM SIBI MVNVS—*A service that is a reward to itself*, p. 61, Emb. 31. Bounty conferring favours on the needy.

MORIR PIV TOSTO CHE MANCAR DI FEDE—*Rather die at once than fail of fidelity*, p. 9, Emb. 5. The Holy Spirit in the heart amidst afflictions.

MVSICA DII PLACANTVR, MVSICA MANES—*By music the gods are appeased, by music the manes*, p. 35, Emb. 18. Music encircled by ears.

NON MANCA AL FIN SE BEN TARDA A VENIRE—*Divine power fails not in the end, though slow to come*, p. 19, Emb. 10. The hand of power, the lion and the wolf.

NVLLVM BONVM INREMVNERATVM — *No good deed unrewarded.* p. 3, Emb. 2. The lion, crowned by Mercury's wand, dispensing justice and plenty.

ORDINE TEMPO NVMERO E MISURO—*Order, time, number, and measure*, p. 37, Emb. 19. Science seated in her chair of state.

PACE A GLI ELETTI E GVERRA A GLI EMPI E REI—*Peace to the chosen, and war to the impious and wicked*, p. 49, Emb. 25. A winged lion holding a sword.

PACE, FERMEZZA E FRVTTO ALL' AIME APPORTO—*Peace, stability, and fruit I bring to the soul*, p. 25, Emb. 13. The sun shining on a fruit-bearing tree.

POST NVBILA PHEBUS—*After clouds the sun*, p. 7, Emb. 4. An eagle bearing Prince Henry's coronet and the crown, the sun shining

QVEL CHE DRITTO DA IL CIEL TORCER NON PVOSSE—*Whatever is straight from heaven cannot be twisted*, p. 17, Emb. 9. A globe upheld by the hand of Providence, and men attempting with ropes to pull the globe aside.

QVI CVRAT VIGILANS DORMIT—*Whoever has charge sleeps watching*, p. 13, Emb. 7. A statesman with a key keeping watch.

QVIS CONTRA NOS ?—*Who against us?* p. 31, Emb. 16. Jove's arm launching thunderbolts.

REX ET SACERDOS DEI—*King and Priest of God*, p. 2, Emb. 1. Crown and mitre on a table.

SERO IVPITER DIPHTHERAM INSPEXIT—*Late hath Jupiter beheld the shepherd's cloak*, p. 43, Emb. 22. The ship of the Roman faith in storms.

SIC VBIQVE—*So everywhere*, p. 63, Emb. 32. Diana with arrow and bow.

SOTT HVMANO SEMBIANTE EMPIO VENENO—*Under human guise impious poison*, p. 39, Emb. 20. The sycophant playing with a cur at his feet.

SVB VMBRA ALARVM TVARVM—*Under the shadow of thy wings*, p. 11, Emb. 6. The sheep pursued by a wolf seeking an eagle's wings.

PEACHAM'S MINERVA. 169

TEMPVS CORONAT INDVSTRIAM—*Time crowns industry*, p. 55, Emb. 28.
Time presenting a wreath to a traveller.
VNICA ETERNA AL MONDO—*The only eternal bird in the world*, p. 5, Emb. 3.
A Phœnix on the funereal fire.
VNVM COR, VNVS DEVS, VNA RELIGIO—*One heart, one God, one religion*,
p. 29, Emb. 15. The hands of Providence clasping a bleeding heart,
within a wreath of laurel, olive, and palm.
VNVM ET ALTERVM DIVINVM—*One and the other*, i. e. *both divine*, p. 45,
Emb. 23. A bud, half rose, half pomegranate.
VIRTVS VNITA FORTIOR—*United virtue the stronger*, p. 59, Emb. 30. A
figure half scholar, half knight.
Without motto, p. 41, Emb. 21. The triple crown surmounting a shield,
within which is displayed Falsehood seated on a seven-headed monster
and presenting her cup of witchery.

A curious, though not very rare volume, Peacham's
MINERVA BRITANNA, 4to, 1612, described at pp. 85–87,
may be looked upon as the herald of the *Mirrovr of
Maiestie*. Published in the same reign, it devotes several
of its Emblems, Mottoes, and Devices to noble personages
who flourished under James I. Some Emblems assumed
by the king, or by his ancestors, we have noted at
pp. 67, 68; and others, suitable to our work, and having
a natural connexion with it, we now select; their Photo-
lith reproductions, and some of Italian and Dutch origin,
constitute the ILLUSTRATIVE PLATES of our volume, and
whether ornamental or not, are undoubtedly appropriate.

I.—From the *Minerva Britanna*, 1612.   See Plate I.

Plate I. The TITLE-PAGE of Peacham's Emblems.
Plate II. p. 1. *Nisi desuper*—Unless from above. To my dread Soveraigne
Iames, King of Great Britaine, &c.
Plate III. p. 11. *Sic pacem habemus*—So have we peace. To the High and
mightie James, King of greate Britaine.
Plate IV. p. 31. *Protegere Regium*—To defend Royalty. JAMES, King of
great Britaine.
Plate V. p. 45. *Hibernica Respub. ad Iacobum Regem*—The Irish Republic
to King James.
Plate VI. p. 145. *Ex vtroque Immortalitas*—Immortality from each. Ad
pijssimum Iacobum magnæ Britanniæ Regem.
Plate VII. p. 13. *In Anna regnantium orbor*—Of those reigning in Anna
the tree. To the Thrice-vertuovs and fairest of Qveenes, Anne Qveene
of Great Britaine.
Plate VIII. p. 18. *E corpore pulchro Gratior*—More beloved from a fair
form. To the RIGHT NOBLE and most towardly Yovng Prince, CHARLES
DVKE OF YORKE.

Plate IX. p. 34. *Ex malis moribus bonæ leges*—Good laws arise from evil manners. To the most iudicious and learned Sir FRANCIS BACON, Knight.
Plate X. p. 20. *His servire*—To serve for these. *To the Right Honourable and my singular good Lord* HENRY HOVVARD, Earle of Northampton, Lord Privie Seale, &c.*
Plate XI. p. 102. *Distantia iungo*—Distant things I unite. To the thrice Noble, and excellent Prince, *Ludowick* Duke of *Lennox*.
Plate XII. p. 21. *Gloria Principum*—The glory of Princes. To the right truely Noble, *and most Honourable Lord*, WILLIAM, *Earle of Pembrooke.*
Plate XIII. p. 23. *His ornari aut mori*—By these to be adorned or to die. *To the right Honourable, and most Noble Lord*, HENRY, *Earle of Southampton.*
Plate XIV. p. 9. *Psalmi Davidici*—Psalms of David. *To the Right Reverend Father in* GOD, IOHN, *Bishop of London.*
Plate XV. p. 28. *His altiora*—Things loftier than these. *To the honourable the Lord Wootton.*

II.—From *Choice Symbols of Heroes*, 1619.
Selectorum Symbolrvm Heroicorvm, &c. See Plate XVI.

A small 8vo Vol. 1.55 d. by .95 ; or 6.1 Eng. in. by 3.14 ; device plates about .55 d. square. There are 1—406 pages numbered, initial 16 and final 26 unnumbered : total, 448 pages.

Contents, pp. (2—13) Dedication, "Illustribvs ac Magnificis Dominis Burgo-grauiis et Baronibus," &c. ; (14, 15) Laudatory verses by Gothardvs Arthvsivs and Ivlivs Gvil. Zincgreffivs ; pp. 1 - 406, "Electorvm Symbolorvm Heroicorvm Centuria Gemina." At the end, p. 26, "Index Herovm," and "Elenchvs Rervm et Verborvm."

The 200 Emblems have each a Latin motto, a well-executed device in a circle, and Latin notes. They are dedicated to various emperors, kings, &c., whom the author supposes to be heroes. The work is of considerable interest, and truly a Mirror of Majesty.

From their relation to our own Reprint, we present a few of the subjects :—

Plate XVI. TITLE-PAGE. Francofvrti, 1619.
Plate XVII. p. 191. HENRICVS VIII Angliæ, Franciæ et Hyberniæ Rex. SECVRITAS ALTERA—*A second safeguard.*
Plate XVIII. p. 193. IDEM. RVTILANS ROSA SINE SPINA—*The red rose without a thorn.*
Plate XIX. p. 195. IACOBVS Angliæ, Galliæ, Scotiæ et Hyberniæ Rex. PRO ME SI MEREOR IN ME—*For me if I deserve against me.*
Plate XX. p. 197. IDEM. NEMO ME IMPUNE LACESSIT—*No one unpunished provokes me.*

---

* Not in the *Mirrovr of Maiestie.*

Plate XXI. p. 199. IACOBVS I STVARTVS Rex Scotiæ. PRO LEGE ET PRO
GREGE—*For law and for people.*
Plate XXII. p. 201. ROBERTVS STVARTVS Rex Scotiæ. VANITAS VANI-
TATVM ET OMNIA VANITAS—*Vanity of vanities, and all things vanity.*
Plate XXIII. p. 207. FRIDERICVS Daniæ, Norvegiæ, Seland. Gothor. Rex.
FEDELTA E COSA RARA—*Fidelity is a rare thing.*
Plate XXIV. p. 209. CHRISTIERNVS SECVNDVS Daniæ, Norvegiæ, Selandiæ,
Goth. Rex. DIMICANDVM—*We must fight.*

III.—From the SENTENTIOUS EMBLEMS of Symeoni, 1560.

A very numerous class of illustrations might be obtained from works in which the Emblems and some heraldic badge, or coat of arms, are blended together. Two or three examples will indicate the nature of such works; they are from the Italian of Gabriel Symeoni, 1509–1570, a Florentine and an historian; and of Battista Pittoni, a painter and engraver, born at Vicenza, in 1508, and still living in 1585. Their volumes are very superior to the *Mirrovr of Maiestie*, but constructed on the same plan of commemorating men of rank and of historic eminence.

LE SENTENTIOSE IMPRESE, &c. *See* Plate XXV.

4to Vol. 2.16 d. by 1.6; or 8.5 Eng. in. by 6.29; full pages 1.45 d. by 1.25; devices .81 d. by 2.04.

REG. a4+4b—q4 13=71 leaves, or 142 pages; unnumbered init. 8, numbered 1—134; total, 142 pages.

CONTENTS (p. 1), Title (2—7), "Al potentissimo et magnanimos. Emanuel Filiberto, Dvca di Savoie, di Ciablaye & di Agosta, Principe di Piamonte, Conte di Brassi, di Nozza & d'Asti, Signor di Vercelli, &c. Gabriel Symeoni felicità continoua & Salute." "In Lione el di xi d' Octobre M.D.LX. Εὐδοκία Magnum magna decent." On 4 pp. "Tavola della Imprese dell' autore." On 1 p. "Nuova Impressa del l'Avtore." On 4 pp. "Avtori allegati nel Dialog.," &c.; pp. 9—124, "TETRASTICHI MORALI."

The Emblems, including the "nvova Impressa," are 127, each with a dedication, a device, motto, and Italian stanza of four lines. The 127 devices are beautifully executed, and consist of an oval design and scroll within a richly-ornamented border. The Photoliths selected are—

Plate XXV. Title-page of "LE SENTENTIOSE IMPRESE."
Plate XXVI. p. 9. Imprese, per I DVCA ET DVCHESSA DI˜SAVOIA.

Plate XXVII. p. 19. DEL RE ET REINA DI NAVARRA.
Plate XXVIII. p. 45. IMPRESSE del Vescovo Giovio, &c. DI CARLO V. IMPERATORE.
Plate XXIX. p. 56. De Papa Lione X.
Plate XXX. p. 127. Del l'Alciato.

IV.—From Pittoni's EMBLEMS OF PRINCES, &c., 1566–1568.

IMPRESE DE DIVERSI PRINCIPE, DVCHI, SIGNORI, &c. *See* Plate XXXI.

Large 4to Vol. 2.75 décim. by 2.03 ; or 10.82 Eng. inches by 7.99. Device plates 2 d. by 1.62. No register nor signatures.
CONTENTS, Pt. I. M.D.LXVI. On 3 pp. a Dedication, "All' illvstre Signore il Conte Hippolito Porto, Condottiere di Gente d' arme della excellentissima Rep. Venetiana." "Battista Pittoni." On 50 leaves as many plates.
Pt. II. M.D.LXVIII. On 1 p. "Al molto Magnifico et excellente S.mio Oss. il S. Cavaliero Giulio Capri." "Di Venetia il x di Giugno MDLXVIII." "Battista Pittoni." On 48 leaves as many plates.

The Impresas or Emblems are 98, each with Device and Motto, Dedication and a Stanza by Lodovico Dolce, well known for his *Dialogo della Pittura*, 8vo, Venezia, 1557; and for his *Vita di Carlo V.*, 4to, in Vinegia, 1567.* Like the *Mirrovr of Maiestie*, Pittoni's *Emblems* have no other text nor explanation. Splendid borders surround the Emblems, which have the mottoes in their centres. There is also a border around each dedication and its stanza.

The following Plates have been selected :—

Plate XXXI. The Title-page of Pittoni's EMBLEMS.
Plate XXXII. p. 3. De l'Imperador Ferdinando I.
Plate XXXIII. p. 29. Qel Capitan Girolamo Mathei Romano.
Plate XXXIV. p. 43. Della Reina di Francia.
Plate XXXV. p. 43. Del S. Titiano Pittore.
Plate XXXVI. Del S. Girolomo Ruscelli.

---

* The fine title-page of this work is one of the numerous ornaments of "THE CHIEF VICTORIES OF THE EMPEROR CHARLES THE FIFTH." By Sir William Stirling-Maxwell, Bart. Large folio. London and Edinburgh, 1870.

V.—From Hillaire's Mirror of Heroes. MDCXIII.

SPECVLVM HEROICVM Principis omnium temporum Poëtarum, HOMERI, &c. *See* Plate XXXVII.

4to Vol. 2.02 décim. by 1.57; or 7.95 Eng. in. by 6.18; full pages 1.65 d. by 1.58; device plates .83 d. by 1.25.
REG. *4 B—G4=28 leaves, unnumbered.
CONTENTS, *1 Title, with Effigies of Homer. *1*v*, Latin, Greek, and French Stanzas on Homer's Effigies, by Marvllvs, Henricvs Stephanvs, and I. Ant. de Baif. *2—4 "Avsonii Bvrdegalensis Viri Con. et Poetæ elegan. ingenii Periochæ (XXIIII) in Iliadem." *4*v*. Portrait and Latin stanza, "Nobilis Vir Isacq. Hilariq. Dm̃s in Riviere Aº 1613." Sig. B1—G4. The 24 plates for the 24 chief events in the 24 books of Homer's Iliad, with a Latin stanza of four lines to each plate. And also with Latin and French descriptive verses below each engraving.

The Plates, finely designed and executed, are by Crispin de Passe, and are in marked contrast with the imperfect type and negligent printing of the letter-press. It is a collection of engravings much sought for, but good copies, like the present, are rare.

The illustrative Photoliths from this work are—

Plate XXXVII. The title of the SPECVLVM HEROICVM.
Plate XXXVIII. Lib. iii. Combat between Paris and Menelaus.
Plate XXXIX. Lib. vi. The conversation of Hector and Andromache.
Plate XL. Lib. xxiv. Achilles, warned by Jove, surrenders the body of Hector.

These works, similar in title and in subject to the *Mirrovr of Maiestie*, would well reward a fuller research and a closer examination. Some of them are peculiarly rich in artistic ornamentation, and manifest how high a place was assigned to the adorning of books intended as well to amuse as to instruct, and to the holding forth of worth and dignity to the admiration of mankind. The purpose was at times much over-wrought, and the characters selected were not always suitable for presentation before a Mirrour of untarnished honour; yet no age of the world will betoken true progress if there shall be no worship of heroes, nor regard for those who are mighty in mental and moral power.

Thus we conclude the fac-simile Reprint of the MIRROVR OF MAIESTIE, a production of little merit in itself, but, from its extreme rarity, deserving a place on the shelves of book-collectors. It has, too, some historical interest, from representing one of the tastes and pursuits of the age in which it appeared.

H. G.

(175)

GENERAL INDEX.

ABBOT, George, Archbishop of Canterbury, Arms and Emb. named, 9, 91; Annotations on, 111; portraits, where, 166.
Achilles surrenders the body of Hector, 178; Emb., Pl. xl.
Admiral, the Lord, *see* Nottingham, Earl of.
Æschylus describes heraldic insignia, 98.
Aikin's *Mem. of Court of James I.*, 91.
Alciat's *Emblems*—Eng. version, 1551, 75; several in Whitney, 80; Yates MS. of, 88.
Alciato, 172; Emb., Pl. xxx.
Ames's *Antiquities of Printing*, 75.
Andrews, Lancelot, Bishop of Ely, Arms and Emb., 44; Annotations on, 140; named, 91; portraits, where, 166.
Anjou, Geoffrey of, his badge *Plantagenista*, 100.
Anne of Denmark, queen of James I., Arms and Emb., 4; Annotations on, 106—109; portraits, where, 161; Emblem of, Pl. vii.
Annotations on the Armorial Bearings and Noble Personages, 97—159.
Armorial distinctions, the earliest, a wolf and a dog, by Anubis and Macedo, 99.
Arms, assumed, 103; the bearing of, allowed by law, Hen. V., 104; the best test of "gentle blood," 104.
Arms of personages in the *Mirrour*, 1—64.
Arms, royal, of Scotland, 165; Denmark, 165; ducal, of Holstein, 165.
Arthur, son of Henry VII., assumed the feather badge, 101.
Arundel, Earl of, Thomas Howard, Arms and Emb., 24; Annotations on, 125; his fame as a collector of art, 91.

BACON, Sir Francis, the Lord Chancellor, Arms and Emb., 10; named, 91; Annotations on, 113; portrait, where, 166; Emb., Pl. ix.
Badges, or personal cognizances.—M. Valerius, 99; Clifford, Warwick, Richard II., &c., 100—102.
Barclay's *Shyp of Folys of the World*, 1509, account of, 73-4.
Barkham, Dr., *Display of Heraldry*, 1601, attributed to him, 85.
Barrington's *Lectures on Heraldry*, 100.
Bellay, *Les Oeuvres du*, 76, 79; translations from, by Spenser, 79.
Bible, *True and Lyvely Portreatures of*, 1553, 75.
Birch's *Heads of Illustrious Personages*, 1743, 163.
Bidpay, or Pilpay, fables, 78.
Black Prince, and badge of ostrich feathers, doubtful if from Crescy, on his tomb at Canterbury, 101.
Boleyn, Queen Anne, her device, 68.
Book-collector, foolish, description of, 73.
Boutell's *Heraldry, Historical and Popular*, 100.
Brandt's *Narren Schyff*, 1494, 73.
Brooke's *Cat. and Succ. of the Kings, &c. of England*, 1622, 164.
Buckingham, Marquess of, George Villiers, Arms and Emb., 20; Annotations on, 122; portraits of, where, 166.
Burke's *Encyclopædia of Heraldry*, 100.
Bylling's *Fyve Wounds of Christ*, 1400, 70.
Bynneman's Translation of Vander Noot's *Theatre*, 1569—Spenser's epigrams, 79.

CANTERBURY, Archbishop of, *see* Abbot.

Carew, the Lord, George Carew, Arms and Emb., 58; Annotations on, 150.
Catalogue of personages unto whom the Mirrovr is appropriated, sign. A2.
Chamberlain, the Lord, *see* Pembroke.
Chancellor, the Lord, *see* Bacon.
Charles V., Emperor, *Twelve Victories of,* 172; Emb., Pl. xxviii.
Charles, Duke of York, Prince of Wales, Emb. and Arms, 6; Annotations on, 109; portraits, where, 166; Emb., Pl. viii.
Chaucer, *Canterbury Tales, Romaunt of the Rose,* Emb., 65; *Well of Love,* 66.
Chief Justices, the three lords, Arms and Emb., 62, 63; Annotations on, 154—158; *see* Hobart, Montagu, and Tanfield.
Christiernus II., king of Denmark, 171; Emb., Pl. xxiv.
Clarendon's *Hist. of Eng.,* 1707, 163.
Coat-armour, or coats of arms, 103.
Cognizances of various nations, 98; kings, 100; and nobles, 101-2.
Coke's test of "gentle blood," 104.
Collier's *Bibliog. and Crit. Cat. of early Eng. Lit.*—on Wyrley, 80; on Willet, 82; on Peacham, 87.
Colours, Emblems for Faith, Hope, Charity, 77, 78.
Combe's *Theater of fine Devises,* 1592, 81; his translation from Perrière, 80.
Complaint of Duke of Buckingham, 160.
Corser, Rev. T., of Stand, his copy of *Mirrovr of Maiestie,* 89; once belonged to Lodge, sold for £36, 93, p. vi.
Cromwell, Lord, his *Impresas,* 86.
Crosse, his *Covert* MS., about 1600, 84.
Crusades, their effect on heraldry, 103.
Crusaders, their cognizances, 103.

DANIELL'S *Worthy Tract of Paulus Iouius,* 1585, 77.
Darcie, the Lord, his Arms and Emb., 52; Annotations on, 148.
Denmark, kings of, Emblems, 69; arms of, 165.
De Strada's *Symbola Div. et Hum.,* 1601, 67.
Diodorus, his notice of military ensigns, 98.
Domenichi's *Ragionamento,* 1556, 77.

Doni's *Mondi,* &c., 1552-3, 78.
Dorset, Earl of, Richard Sackville, Arms and Emb., 32; notice of, 91.
Dorset, Earl of, Thomas Sackville,—Misery, Sleep, and Old Age, 67; extraordinary man of genius, 91; Annotations on, 132.
Drawing and Limning, 1612, Peacham's, 87.
Drayton's *Legends,* 1596, 95; dedication of his *Odes,* 1619, to Sir Henry Goodere, 95-6.
Dugdale's *Monasticon Ang.,* testimony to Lydgate, 72.
Dunbar's *Dance of the Seven Deadly Sins*—Pride, 66.
Dyalogus Creaturarum, 1480, 74.

EDWARD I., II., and III., Edward the Black Prince, Edward VI., their Emblems, 68, 86, 87.
Edward IV., a faulcon in fetterlock, 100; the sun in splendour, 101.
Elizabeth's badges and mottoes, 68.
Ely, Bishop of, *see* Andrews.
Emblem-books, English, previous to A.D. 1618, 65—96.
Emblems in early English poets, 65, 66.
Emblems, *thirty-two* in the *Mirrovr of Maiestie,* 167; Mottoes and Devices, 167—169.
England's Eliza, 160.
English Sovereigns and their Emblems, 67-8.
English Nobles and Gentry, and their Emblems, 69.
English Versions of Emblem books—Brandt's, 1509, 73; *Dial. of Creatures,* 74; *Portreatures of the woll Bible,* 1553; *Images of the Old Testament,* 1549; *Storys and Prophesis,* 1535; of Alciat, 1551; *Tryumphes of Petrarcke,* 1560, 75; *Visions,* by Spenser, 76; *Worthy Tract of Paulus Iouius,* 77; North's *Morall Philosophie of Doni,* 1570; Paradin's *Heroicall Devises,* 1591, 78; Bynneman's *Theatre,* 1569, 79; *Emblemes of Love,* 85; Alciat, about 1600, MS., 88.
Essex, Earl of, Robert Devereux, Arms and Emb., 30; Annotations on, 131; Emblems noted, 86; among "Illustrious

GENERAL INDEX.

and Heroyicall Princes," 91; portrait, where, 166.
Exercise, the Gentleman's, 1612, 87.

FAERNO, Gabriel, quoted in Whitney, 80.
Feather badge, account of, 101.
Ferdinando I., Emperor, 172; Emb., Pl. xxxii.
Fewterer's *Myrrour of Christ's Passion*, 161.
France, Queen of, 172; Emb., Pl. xxxiv.
Fraunce's *Insignium*, &c., 1588, 80.
Fredericus, king of Denmark, 171; Emb., Pl. xxiii.
Fuller's *Worthies*—praise of Willet, 81.

G. (H.), initials of the author of the *Mirrovr*, interpreted to be the ciphers of Sir Henry Goodere, 93, 94, 95; signature also to the Reprint, 96.
Gaunt, John of, alluded to, 100.
Giovio's *Dialogo*, 77.
Glasse for Gamesters, 161.
Goodere, Sir Henry, supposed author of the *Mirrovr*, 93, 94, 95, 96.
Granger's *Biog. Hist. of Eng.*, 1799, 163.
Green's *Mirrour for the Ladies of England*, 161; *Penelope's Web*, 161.
Green's reprint of Whitney, 80.
Guguin's *Mirouer historial de France*, 1516, 161.
Guillim's *Display of Heraldry*, 1610, 85.

HASLEWOOD'S *Dial. of Creatures moralysed*, 1816, 74.
Haye, the Lord James, Arms and Emb., 60; Annotations on, 152.
Hazlitt's, W. C., *Handbook of Early Eng. Lit.*—on Bynneman, 79; on Combe, 81; on Peacham, 85; on *Mirrovr of Maiestie*, 89; on its authorship, 93.
Hector and Andromache, conversation, 173; Emb., Pl. xxxix.
Henry I., II., IV., V., VII., and VIII., of England, their Emblems, 67, 68, 86.
Henry VIII., Emb., 170; Pl. xvii. and xviii.
Herald and emblematist in close alliance, 78.

Heraldic blazonry systematized, 102; of use in the Crusades, 103.
Heraldic symbolism in extensive use, 97, 98; of ancient adoption, 98.
Heraldry uses the same as Emblems, 97; an organized system, as in badges, 99.
Hertford, Earl of; Edward Seymour, Arms and Emb., 28; Annotations on, 129.
Hic, hæc, hoc taceatis, saying of Edmund of Langley, 101.
Hillaire's *Speculum Heroicum Homeri, &c.*, 1613, 173; Emb. Pl. Title, xxxvii.; other Plates, xxxviii.—xl.
Hobart, Sir Henry, Lord Chief Justice of Common Pleas, Arms and Emb., 62; Annotations on, 155.
Holland's *Booke of Kings*, 1618, 162; list of portraits named, 162.
Holland's *Book of Heroes*, 1620, 163.
Honour in its Perfection, 1624, 91.
Howard, Thomas, see Earl of Suffolk.
Huth's, Mr., copy of *Mirrovr of Maiestie*, 89; *Poetical Miscellanies*, 93.

IMPRESAS of Englishmen, 86; Symeoni's *Sententiose Imprese*, 171; Pittoni's *Imprese di diversi Principi*, &c., 172.
Induction, the, by Thomas Sackville, 160.

JAMES I., of England, taste for Emblems, 70; Arms and Emb., 1, 2, 3; Annotations on, 105; Arms and Mottoes, 164, 169, 170; portraits, where, 162, 166; Emblems of, Pl. ii. —vi., xiv., xx.
James III., of Scotland, and IV. and V., Embs., 70; portraits mentioned, 165.
James I., of Scotland, portrait, 165; Emb., 171, Pl. xxi.
Jesus the Well of grace, 70, 71.
Junius, Hadrian, Emblems in Whitney, 80.

KEIR (Scotland), most extensive Emblem-book library there, 75.
Kent, Joan of, Emb. a white hart, 100.
King, the, see James I., of England.
King, John, see Bishop of London.
Knights, names and arms of, 1485—1624, 69.

GENERAL INDEX.

LANCASTER, John of, 87.
Langley, Edmund, impress, a falcon in a fetterlock, 100.
Leeu, Gerard, of Gouda, 74.
Leigh's *Accidens of Armory*, 1562, 79.
Leigh, Sir Henry, his Emblems, 86.
Lennox, Duke of, Lodowick Stuart, Arms and Emb., 18; Annotations on, 120; Chamb. and Admiral of Scotland, 91; portrait, where, 166; Emb., 170, Pl. xi.
Lennox, Duchess of, portrait, where, 164.
Leo X., 172; Emb., Pl. xxix.
Le Vasseur's *Devises des Empereurs Romains*, 1608, 67.
Lisle, Lord Viscount, Robert Sidney, Arms and Emb., 36; Annotations on, 136; brother of Sir P. Sidney, 91.
Lodge's *Portraits of Illust. Persous of Gt. Britain*—notice of the *Mirrovr*, 92, 93; title, 163.
London, Bishop of, John King, 91; Arms and Emb., 41; Annotations on, 138; no motto, 89; portrait. where. 166; Emb., 170, Pl. xiv.
Looking-glass for England, 161; *Ireland*, 161.
Lorenzo the Magnificent,—his symbol of Faith, Hope, Charity, 77.
Lunettes des Princes, 1493, 162.
Lydgate's *Dance of Macaber*, 66; account of, 71; *Life and Death of Hector*, 71; knowledge of Emblems, — St. Edmund's banner, 72.

MACHABRE, Daunce of, 1541, 71; set up at St. Paul's, Henry VI.—pulled down in 1549, 71.
Magistrates, Mirror of, Lord Sackville's description of Misery, &c., 67.
Mary, Queen, her emblems, 68.
Meres' *Wits Commonwealth*, names several emblematists, 81.
Miror des escoliers, 161.
Mirouer historial de France, 161.
Mirour of Monsters, 160.
Mirovr for Magistrates, 160.
Mirrhor, mete for all Mothers, &c., 160.
Mirror great variety of works with this title, 159-161.
Mirror of Magistrates, 67.
Mirror, Mariners, 161.
Mirror of Martyrs, 160.
Mirrouer des femmes vertueuses, 161.
Mirroure of Gold, 159.
Mirrour, Ideas, 161.
Mirrour for the Ladies, 161.
Mirrour of Madness, 159.
Mirrovr for Man, 159.
Mirrour of his Maiesties present government, 161.
Mirrovr of Mutabilitie, 160.
Mirrovr of Policie, 1598, 83.
Mirrovr of Princely deeds, 161.
Mirrovr of Maiestie, 1618, Title, Dedication, and Catalogue of Names, A1-A4; Arms and Emblems, 1-63; rarity of, 89; thirty-three coats of arms, thirty-two emblems, twelve Knights of the Garter, 89; rank of the persons, 90; estimate of the work, 90; bishops, officers of State, and other nobles, 91; Lodge's account of the work, 92; Corser's copy used for this reprint, 93; authorship, 93—96.
Montagu, James, *see* Bishop of Winchester.
Montagu, Sir Henry, Lord Chief Justice of King's Bench,—arms, 62; named, 91; Annotations on, 154; portrait, where, 167.
Montgomery, Earl of, Philip Herbert, Arms and Emb., 34; Annotations on, 134; *Amorvm Emblemata*, 1608, dedicated to, 85; portrait, where, 166.
More, Sir Thomas, Emblems by him, 72; their subjects, 73—86.
Mottoes and Emblems of English Sovereigns, 67-8, 100; of the *Mirrovr of Maiestie*, 167-8; from the *Minerva Britanna*, 169; from *Selectorvm Symbolorum*, 170; from Symeone's *Imprese*, 171; from Pittoni's *Imprese*, 172; from Hillaire's *Specvlvm Heroicvm*, 173.
Myrror, Christall, or Penelope's Web, 161.
Myrrour of Christ's Passion, 161.
Myrrour of good Maners, 1516, 74.
Myrrour of the Worlde, 161.

NAVARRE, King and Queen of, 172; Emb., Pl. xxvii.
Neugebaverus, his *Select. Symbolorvm Heroicvm*, 1619, 67—69; Illustrative

GENERAL INDEX. 179

Plates from, namely Pl. xvi., xvii., xviii., xix., xx., xxi., xxii., xxiii., and xxiv.
orth's *Morall Philosophie of Doni*, 1570, 78.
orthampton, Earl of, Henry Howard, 170; Emb., Pl. x.
ottingham, Earl of, Charles Howard, Arms and Emb.,—Lord Admiral, 16, 91; Annotations on, 119.; *Winter Night's Vision*, 160; portrait, where, 166.

OLD TESTAMENT, the Images of, 1549, 75.
rmond, courageous, Lisle and Say, 87.

PARADIN'S *Devises heroiques*, 1557, translated into Eng., 1591, 78; in Whitney, 80.
ris and Menelaus, combat between, 173; Emb., Pl. xxxviii.
rker's *Tryumphes of Fraunces Petrarcke*, 1560, 75.
acham's *Minerva Britanna*, testimony to Eng. emblems, 69, 70, 86; various works of his, 86—88; plates illustrative of the *Mirrovr of Maiestie*, from *Minerva Britanna*, list of, 169, 170, Pl. i. Title, and ii. to xv. inclusive.
mbroke, Earl of, William Herbert, Lord Chamberlain; Arms and Emb., 22, 91; Annotations on, 124; *Amorvm Emblemata*, 1608, dedicated to, 85; portrait, where, 166; Emb., 170, Plate xii.
nelope's Web, 161.
rgaminus, N., author of *Dyalogus* CREATURARUM, 14th cent., 74.
rrière's *Theatre des bons Engins*, 1539, fragment of a transl., 75; Were Combe's Emblems from this? 81.
rsonal heraldic signs or cognizances, 99.
trarcha, *Gli Triumphi del*, 1500, translated into English 1560, 75; Visions, 76.
œnix, the, from Petrarch, 76.
pay, or Bidpay, fables of, 78.
toni's *Imprese di Diversi Principi, &c.*, 72; title, Pl. xxxi.
ntagenista, emblem of humility, borne by Geoffrey of Anjou, 100; whence Plantagenets, 100.

Portraits named in *Ornamental Heraldry*, 165.
Portraits of personages in *Mirrovr of Maiestie*, where found, 166.
Prince, the, *see* Charles I.
Privy seal, the, *see* Worcester, Earl of.

QUADRIN'S *Hist. de la Bible*, and Eng. version, 1553, 75.
Queen, the, *see* Anne of Denmark.

REUSNER, an Emblematist, 81.
Richard II., Emblem and Motto, 68; favourite badge, a white hart, 100.
Robert Stuart, 171; Emb., Pl. xxii.
Romano, Captain G. M., 172; Emb., Pl. xxxiii.
Ruscelli's *Discorso*, 1556, 77; *Imprese illustre*, 77; Pittoni's Emb. of, 172, Pl. xxxvi.

S. (P.), *Heroicall Devises*, 1591, 78.
Sackville, Richard and Thomas, *see* Dorset, Earl of.
Sambucus, Emblematist, in Whitney, 80, 81.
Savoy, Duke and Duchess of, 171; Emb., Pl. xxvi.
Say, named, 87.
Scotland, Kings of—Emblems named, 69; given in Pl. xix.—xxii.; Arms of, named, 165; Arms impaled with those of Denmark, 165.
Scotland, *Lawes and Actes of Parl. of*, 1597, 166.
Sendebar, Parables of, 78.
Seymour, Edward, *see* Hertford, Earl of.
Shakespeare's allusions to cognizances, 101, 102.
Shield, embellished, 98.
Sidney, Sir P., *Covntesse of Pembroke's Arcadia* shows knowledge of emblems, 69; *see also* 77, 86, 91.
Southampton, Earl of, Henry Wriothesley, Arms and Emb., 26; Annotations on, 128; Shakespeare's friend, 91; account of, by Lodge, 92; portraits, where, 166; Emb., 170, Pl. xiii.
Spectacle for Perjurers, 161.
Speght's *Workes of Chaucer*, 1598, 71.

Spenser's *Visions*, Calender, &c., 76—79.
Stanhope, the Lord John, Arms and Emb., 56; Annotations on, 149.
Steuarta, Elisabetha, anagram, *Has Artes beata valet*, 86.
Stirling-Maxwell, Sir William, Bart., his *Chief Victories of the Emperor Charles the Fifth*, 69, 172; possesses a relic of Combe's Emb., 81; *Ornamental Heraldry*, 165. See Keir.
Storys and Prophesis, 1535, 75.
Stuart, Lodowick, *see* Lennox, Duke of.
Suffolk, Earl of, Thomas Howard, the Lord Treasurer, Arms and Emb., 12; named, 91; Annotations on, 115—166.
Symeoni's *Sententiose Imprese*, 1560, 171; Title, Pl. xxv.; other Pl. xxvi.—xxx.

TANFIELD, Sir Laurence, Lord Chief Baron of the Exchequer—Arms, 62, 63; Annotations on, 157.
Theatre des bons Engins, see Perrière.
Titian, Painter, 172; Emb., Pl. xxxv.
Treasurer, the Lord, *see* Suffolk, Earl of.

VÆNIUS, Otho, his *Amorvm Emblemata*, Lat., It., and Eng. verses, 1608, 85.
Vander Noot's *Theatre, &c.*, 1568, Eng. version, 1569, 79.
Villiers, George, *see* Buckingham.

WALES, Prince of, and feather badge, 101.
Wallingford, the Lord Viscount, William Knolles, Arms and Emb., 38; Annotations on, 137; portrait, where, 166.

Watson's *Shyppe of Fooles*, 1509, 73.
Wentworth, the Lord, Arms and Emb. 50; Annotations on, 144.
Whitney's *Emblemes*, 1586, 79; the print contains Willet's *first emble* 80–82; Crosse's *Covert*, 84.
Willet's *Sacrorvm Emb. Cent. vna*, 8 acrostic and quotation, 82.
William I. of England, Emb. and Mot 67.
Winchester, Bishop of, Montagu, Jam Arms and Emb., 42; named, 91; A notations on, 139; portrait, whe 166.
Windsor, the Lord, Arms and Emb., 4 Annotations on, 143.
Winter-night's Vision, 160.
Worcester. Earl of, Edward Somers Lord Privy Seal, Arms and Emb., 91; Arms and Annotations on, 11 portrait, where, 166.
Wotton, the Lord, Arms and Emb., 5 Annotations on, 149; Emb., 171, xv.
Wruthesley, Henry, *see* Southampt Earl of.
Wyatt's *Turns of Fortune*, 66.
Wyrley's *True Vse of Armorie*, 15 80.

YATES, J. B., on Fraunce's *Insign* 80; MS. of *Eng. Transl. of Alc* 88.
Yorke's *Vnion of Honovr*, 1640, 164.

ZOUCH, the Lord, Arms and Em 46; Annotations on, 141.

Wyman & Sons, Printers, Great Queen Street, London, W.C.

LaVergne, TN USA
16 May 2010
182840LV00002B/102/A